Praise for Cindy Clark and
PAW PAW SECRETS

"Can't wait to read the next one!" —*Early Reader Review*

"What a great story and a stellar job." —*Early Reader Review*

"I loved the book . . . This would make a great TV, movie, or even a series. It is a unique concept." —*Early Reader Review*

"Kept me guessing . . . hard to put down."
—*Early Reader Review*

About the Author

Cindy Clark is new to fiction writing. Most of her life has been spent writing non-fiction, either as a lawyer or as an executive in the biotechnology industry. The pandemic offered plenty of time to write, and she has fulfilled her lifelong dream to publish a fiction novel. Cindy graduated from Wesleyan University, with degrees in mathematics and government, and has her law degree from Washington College of Law, American University. She loves music and has performed with bands, orchestras and choirs around the US. Most recently, she was a founding member of the Motley Tones. She has also been a long-time volunteer for the Carolina Great Pyrenees Rescue, fostering more than a hundred rescue Pyrs (of course, not all at one time).

PAW PAW SECRETS

A House That Sam Built Mystery

CINDY CLARK

PAW PAW SECRETS

A House That Sam Built Mystery

CINDY CLARK

PAW PAW SECRETS (1st Edition)
A House That Sam Built Mystery

Paperback: 9798988693901
Ebook/Kindle: 9798988693918

Author: Cindy Clark

Cover and interior design by
Eric Williams (@eric5310pub)

With the legal disclaimer out of the way, it is important to note that this book is a work of fiction. Unless noted in the author's notes at the end of the book, the people, places, and events are all fictional. Any similarities to them are a figment of the author's imagination and purely coincidental and unintentional. The main character, Sam, however, is loosely based on the author's brother. He really did build a log home for their parents in West Virginia. But he is much funnier. If you want to know more about the true stuff, be sure to spend a few minutes and read the author's notes at the end before you move on to your next book.

Chapter 1

BASE CAMP

*Base camp: a central place from which activities
or expeditions can be carried out.*

*What do you call a group of crows out camping?
Murder within tent.*

End of September 1994

A heart-stopping scream ripped me from a fretful sleep. My eyes opened and I stared up at the pitch black of the tent. My heart was pounding from the adrenaline. I waited for the disorientation to pass. I was always disoriented when I woke up in a bed that was not my own. I wondered if I dreamed that sound or if it was real.

I listened hard but heard no sounds at all. No breeze, no crickets, no rustling of animals moving around at night. The hillside, just teetering on fall, was holding its breath. Then the sound came again. It was the sound of metal on metal. An ear-splitting, fingernails-on-blackboard, hateful sound so out of place in the quiet woods of West Virginia overlooking the south branch of the Potomac River.

The sound of scraping metal echoed back and forth through the canyon made between the mountains by the river. Distorted and amplified, it was impossible to tell where the sound was coming from.

My new wife, Anna, and I arrived a few days ago. We were preparing the twenty-acre lot for a new log home that we were building as a family project for my parents' retirement. We could pitch our tents down along the river's edge or up on a knoll where the house was going to be. The knoll was more difficult to access due to the thick brush. And snakes. I hated snakes.

Along the river meant we could be closer to our vehicles, but it could flood. Anna worried that a flash flood could sweep the campsite away while we slept. I didn't want my new wife to worry.

We hacked a path to the knoll about one hundred feet

up from the river and made camp. The heavy equipment to cut in the driveway and dig the foundation was due to arrive in a few days. We could move the vehicles up then.

I was surprised the two golden retriever puppies were not barking. Zoey and Zeus, we called them. Collectively referred to as the Z goldens. They were five and seven months old, respectively. They had been thoroughly enjoying cuddling with my wife and me in our sleeping bags. They were staring at me, alert and waiting for my reaction. Maybe it was because this was a new place. Or maybe they didn't interpret the sound as a threat.

I, however, construed the sound as a threat. But like the dogs, I remained quiet. Until I knew what this was, better not to draw attention to ourselves. I slipped out from my sleeping bag and the warm weight of the dogs. I put on my coat and picked up my shotgun leaning by the tent flap. And a flashlight.

And my cell phone. One of the original Nokia phones. It was 8" x 3" and almost two inches thick. A brick. In 1994, there was no cell service in these sparsely populated mountains. Basically, all the phone did was make phone calls. It didn't take photos. You could not search the internet. The screen was less than one-quarter of the size of the phone. You could barely read two lines of characters.

Granted, this was a huge upgrade from my car phone. It was billed as portable, but at 18" x 12" x 4" and carried around in a big bag with a shoulder strap, it was hardly portable. It also didn't have a built-in antenna. The antenna was mounted on the roof of the van. If you were not next to the van, no reception. As I said, the Nokia was light years ahead of my old behemoth car phone.

I entered 911 in case this noise was an emergency requiring outside intervention and I could find a sliver of service somewhere.

I put my finger to my lips in the universal sign to *shhhh*. I could see in my wife's eyes she had a hundred questions that she was ready to let fly. Did you hear that noise? What was it? What should we do? Anna nodded and said nothing. We had only been married a couple of months, but I could already read her like a book.

Unasked question number 101, were you seriously going to leave me here by myself? I gave the universal hand signal for "stay." In my mind, the meaning was clear. Stay in the tent. I left the puppies to keep her company while I went to find the answers to her other unasked questions.

With only the stars and a sliver of a moon lighting my way, I moved quietly down the hill and arrived at the road that ran adjacent to the river. Everything was perfectly still. I looked left and right for light or sounds of the origin of the noise. Nothing. I turned on the flashlight. And then I saw it, or more accurately, I didn't see it.

My wife's car, which was parked along the road, was missing. It was a huge boat of a beater car, at least fifteen years old and covered in rust. Her first car, the Cadillac, complete with side wings, was her parents' idea of how to keep her safe. We wanted them to keep it. But no. They insisted we take it.

We had parked it over the top of the hitch of the trailer that hauled my four-wheel ATV we were planning to use on the jobsite. I figured that would foil the plans of any enterprising redneck from a quick grab and dash to steal the trailer and four-wheeler. I have to say, that plan worked great. The trailer and four-wheeler were still in place. Anna's car, however, was MIA.

I reached into the pocket of my coat and found the keys to my work van. At least now I didn't have to go back up the hill. I checked the cell phone. No service.

I jumped in the van and headed in the direction of known cell service coverage about four miles away so I could call the police. Adrenaline pumping, I gripped the steering wheel, the tires slipping slightly on the gravel.

As I rounded a switchback curve in the road where the road moved away from the river and headed up into the hills, I slammed on the brakes, barely stopping in time. I nearly collided with a hulking black object completely blocking the narrow road. Anna's car.

I turned off the engine and jumped out of the van. I walked around Anna's car, trying all the doors. They were locked. I didn't have Anna's car keys in my coat pocket. Anna did, back at the tent with the puppies.

I saw that the front bumper of Anna's car was missing. The bumper was a huge hunk of solid metal only found on really old cars. Nothing like the plastic crumple bumpers on the newer cars the manufacturers were churning out in the 1990s.

I jogged up the road to see what was ahead. Maybe the thieves were regrouping to come back to get the car. Something reflected the thin light of my flashlight about a hundred feet away. It was the bumper.

At least we didn't have to put in an insurance claim. I wondered if Anna even had insurance on this thing. As her husband, I probably should have known the answer to this question.

And I didn't have to confront the thieves. That would

have been bad.

I would have preferred that the thieves had successfully managed to haul the car away. Would have saved me the trip to the salvage yard. Looked like they tried to drag the car by the bumper. But the bumper fell off because it was so rusted. Just my luck. And theirs.

Because the road was so narrow, I couldn't get around Anna's car. I looked at my phone. The time, 2 a.m., glowed back up at me, but no cell service bars. In this remote area, there were only a few houses scattered along the road. We hadn't formally introduced ourselves to the neighbors yet. Correction, we did meet one neighbor in the woods while we were trenching in the electric line at the back of the property the day before.

My wife was in the driver's seat of the trencher because we kept running into rocks. I had to dig them out while she operated the controls. I really wanted to run the machine. It would have been so much fun. But making Anna dig out the rocks didn't seem to be a good allocation of duties.

Anna was tall for a woman. She was slim and athletic with long black hair. Her strength amazed me. I've seen her take a twelve-foot, fifty-pound log, balance it over one shoulder and walk it fifty feet without breaking a sweat. She didn't even go to the gym to work out with weights. Must have been good peasant stock. It was no wonder I married this woman.

Despite her strength, she needed almost half an hour to dig out the first rock. Just kidding. I didn't make her dig out rocks. The main reason was that I was looking forward to getting the trenching job done as soon as possible. Then we could enjoy newly married activities in the woods, like eating pork and beans heated over the campfire and throwing the ball for the puppies.

So Anna got to have all the fun on the tractor. And some fun later, off the tractor. Ah, the sacrifices you make for your spouse.

Over the sound of the trencher motor, we heard someone yelling. My wife turned the motor off. A man appeared out of nowhere, wearing a blaze orange vest.

He looked up at my wife and said, "How's it hanging?"

She was wearing this silly fishing hat with flaps on the sides and jean overalls. Her hair was stuffed up under the hat. When she looked up, the hat slipped off her head and her long black hair spilled down her back.

She and I both said, "What?" at the same time, but with entirely different inflections.

Anna's "what" was that of someone who didn't hear what you said. Her ears were still ringing from the sound of the motor.

Mine was one of the incredulous. That was an extremely inappropriate way for a stranger to address my new wife.

"Oh, I'm sorry, I thought you were a man," he said.

I didn't think she looked like a man at all, but I could undress her with my eyes, so I figured I was biased. Maybe the guy was nearsighted.

Construction equipment brought men out from the woodwork to see what was going on, whether you were in New York City or the backwoods of West Virginia. The noise we made probably echoed off the mountains for miles.

"I'm Curtis. I live on the other side of the mountain,"

the man said, vaguely pointing back over his shoulder. "My family's been hunting this land for a few generations. I'd heard they sold it off to a developer."

"It's great to meet you, Curtis," I said, ignoring the subtle not-from-around-here jab.

"Where's the house site going to be?" Curtis asked.

I climbed out of the six-foot-deep trench and walked over to Curtis. "We're putting the house on the rise overlooking the river," I said.

Curtis and I turned to each other in that age-old male-bonding ritual. I was aware of the dagger eyes directed my way from Anna, who was sitting alone on top of the trencher. But she smiled a huge Cheshire cat smile and listened. I knew I would hear about this later, even though it was not my fault. I sent her mental images of all the fun things we were going to do that evening. Pork and beans. Throw the ball.

"Have you started digging anywhere else on the property?" Curtis asked.

What, was the guy worried about Indian burial grounds? It would have come up on the title search, right?

"No, not yet. We thought we'd get a head start on the trench while we wait for the heavier equipment to put in the driveway and dig the foundation," I said.

"Well, I won't keep you from your work," said Curtis. "See you around." He melted back into the woods. And we continued digging.

In theory, I could go to Curtis's house to use his phone to report the crime. Since we were neighbors and I knew him, kind of. He seemed like the type of guy who would help another guy out when his wife's car was dragged a mile down the road and left there in the middle of the night.

Curtis's house was on "the other side of the mountain," exact location unspecified. Probably difficult to find in the dark. And he probably had a gun.

Any hope of finding the vile perpetrators of the heinous car-dragging was quickly evaporating. The known cell service point was about a thirty-minute walk from where I stood at Anna's car.

But I didn't feel good about leaving the car in the middle of the road in case someone leaving at dark o'clock for an early shift might not be as observant as I was and run into Anna's car, abandoned by thieves and blocking the road.

Nothing left to do but start knocking on doors. At 2 a.m. In the pitch dark. In West Virginia. Where people have been known to shoot first and ask questions later.

I was 6 feet tall, 180 pounds, broad-shouldered and well-muscled from years of working construction. My unbrushed curly brown hair could use a trim. If I knocked on my door at 2 a.m., I wouldn't answer. Or I'd shoot. I had to go back and get Anna.

I found her at the bottom of the hill next to the road with a flashlight and the puppies. Apparently, the universally understood hand signal for "stay" could be liberally interpreted to mean don't go where I was going but feel free to roam about when danger was lurking. *How could she put the puppies at risk like this?* I kept this thought to myself.

I gave her the blow-by-blow. Your car was stolen. The bumper fell off down the street. I found your car and your bumper. I didn't get shot and haven't shot anyone. We need to call the police and get your car back here.

I contemplated the options for how to tell her she had to be the one to knock on a neighbor's door.

I could use the expendable argument. My parents' entire life savings was on the line. If someone shot me, there would be no way we could get this house built. On the other hand, as you know, your main role was to fulfill my every need. Nope, couldn't say that.

Your main role was to cook and clean. Nope, not that one, either.

Your main role was to assist in the construction activities. That was better. In the event you were shot, we could always find someone else to help. That was not going to work.

I dreaded the conversation. But not as much as the one we had shortly after we were engaged.

Anna and I met at a conference in Chicago. I was there to see some of the construction equipment manufacturers. Anna had been hired as a day worker at one of the trade show booths. I lingered, flirting with her. I convinced her to have dinner with me. We discovered we were both from Michigan. At twenty-five, she was five years my junior.

She had an associate's degree in accounting. Unable to find work in Michigan, where she was still living with her parents, she left her home state to find a job. She was sharing an apartment in Chicago while she looked for full-time work. We dated for six months, taking turns traveling back and forth from Michigan to Illinois.

I was living with my buddy, Frank, in an old fixer-upper

farmhouse we were renting from his uncle. We bartered the rent for construction services on his house.

In 1994, the economy was just coming out of a recession. Michigan had generally been behind the curve in terms of recovery. Unemployment was around 6%. I was struggling to get my business off the ground and had been working non-stop, either for myself or for someone else, with no vacations for ten years.

My father, Nick, was a highway engineer. Yvonne, my mother, was a nurse. Both in their late sixties, they had lived their entire lives in Kalamazoo, Michigan. Tired of the cold winters, they decided to move farther south for their retirement. They wanted someplace with water and mountains. West Virginia fit the bill.

They looked for almost a year for a house that was already built but found nothing. My father started looking at house plans. I don't know how, but he became fascinated with log homes.

He saw this story about a huge log home estate in Michigan called Granot Loma, a 20,000+ square-foot estate that sold for $4.5 million in 1987. It was built by an American businessman in 1919 as a summer residence for his family. He named the vacation home in the Upper Peninsula (which locals called the "UP") by taking random letters from his wife's and children's names.

My parents had a small nest egg saved, so they were looking for the Granot Loma feel at about what they could get for their current home in Kalamazoo, Michigan, a modest three-bedroom they had lived in for thirty years.

Nick found some log home plans and made his own adjustments. Three bedrooms, 2,400 square feet. He showed them to me one night when I was over for dinner. He said they just had to find a lot and a builder.

They found a reasonably priced twenty-acre, mostly wooded lot overlooking the South Branch of the Potomac River in a new development. The residents and lot owners so far were retirees who had lived in Washington, D.C, about four hours away. Professionals like themselves from different parts of the country.

I thought about how they were going to find a good builder. Hard to do in an area you know well. Nearly impossible to find someone you trusted if you were not local. I got caught up in the log home dream. It was then I offered to build them the house.

Since I hadn't had a vacation in a decade, it would be like a work/play thing for a year in the mountains. They were happy to pay me for the year. I gave them the family rate, figuring I could pick up side jobs to supplement my income and it would save them some money. Like Granot Loma, maybe it was a house that we could pass on to the future Bradley generations.

The plan for future Bradley generations became more concrete when I met Anna. But she was a little late to plan for the house-building project. Everything was already set. I upset the applecart when I asked her to marry me.

Me: "Honey, I love you. I can't wait to get married. I have this job in West Virginia building a house for my parents. I am leaving for nine to twelve months. Will you be okay staying here in Chicago? I'll come back to see you when I can."

Her: "Hell no, I go where you go."

Me: "But we are going to be sleeping rough in the woods with no bathroom or shower, and every day we'll be working on the house."

Her: "Great, I'm in. I'll do almost anything to get out of here."

I think that and my body were the main reasons she married me.

"It'll be a great adventure," she said.

Me: "Including servicing my needs on a daily basis?" No, I didn't say that. I'd get that commitment in the marriage vows, right?

My parents added wages for Anna as a helper, and she offered to account for the building project expenses and materials. She would get on-the-job construction training from yours truly. Win-win.

We got married at the end of June in Michigan in the UP. I had a little money saved up, which we blew on a two-week honeymoon in Hawaii. Honestly, we probably could have stayed in Michigan because we hardly left the honeymoon suite. Got a great head start on that future Bradley generation.

When we got back, we packed up Anna's apartment. I moved out of Frank's uncle's place. We bought supplies for our year of living in the woods and headed south to West Virginia.

Getting back to how I was going to tell Anna she had to knock on doors in the middle of the night in West Virginia, I considered the "protect your man" argument. She wouldn't want me to get shot, would she? I hoped she loved me enough to give up her life for me. Felt a little too early in our marriage to ask.

I thought about the "it's your car, so you should do it" argument. That one had possibilities. Plus, I needed her to drive her car back while I drove the van.

I chickened out and decided not to tell her she had to do the knocking until we got to her car. Right time, right place. And it was possible that another angle would occur to me on the way.

We loaded the pups into the van and drove to her car. When we got there, I saw that Anna was boiling mad at the injustice. Angered by the violation of someone dragging her car a mile down the road and then leaving it there. It was her first up-close-and-personal experience with a crime. Bound to leave a mark.

Without hesitation, she jumped out of the van, handed me the dogs' leashes, squared off her shoulders, and walked boldly up to the closest house, all shuttered up and dark. Without my even having to ask her. Dodged the proverbial bullet there. I worshiped this woman. So many hidden talents.

She pounded on the door. No answer. She pounded louder and said in her sweetest, most helpless female voice: "Please, I need help." No answer. But the light on the porch of the house two doors down went on.

A middle-aged man with a beer belly opened the door and stepped onto the porch. "Is someone hurt? Has there been an accident?" he asked. "I heard the commotion."

I saw he was not holding a gun. I breathed a sigh of relief. Anna stepped down off his neighbor's porch so she was not yelling across the yards. She walked to the base of his stairs and looked up at him.

"I'm sorry to disturb you in the middle of the night. We're building a new house a few lots down from you. Someone tried to steal our car," Anna said, pointing to the rust bucket. "I don't have any cell service, and I was wondering if you could call the police."

A woman wearing a housecoat and slippers appeared at the door behind the neighbor. "Barney, what's going on? It's the middle of the night," she said. I was relieved that she was also not holding a gun. Another bullet dodged.

"It's okay, dear. Our new neighbors have had some trouble. They want to use the phone to call the police," said Barney.

"Well, then, don't leave them standing on the stoop," said Lydia Franklin, Barney's wife.

As we stood in their foyer, Anna explained what little we knew.

"Bless your hearts," said Lydia.

It was the first time I had heard that expression. From her inflection and the look in her eyes, I understood that she pitied us. We did look pretty pitiful at 2 a.m., standing on their front stoop.

The correct usage of "bless your heart" was mansplained to this damned Yankee a while later by one of our other neighbors, Cherry.

It could be used either immediately before or immediately after to excuse something bad you said about someone. For example: that guy is an asshole, *bless his heart.*

Or it could be used for someone who was sick: he's got the flu, *bless his heart.* I assumed this was the context in which Lydia made the statement. *What a tough job you had ahead of you building that house, and how awful it was that someone did this to your car.*

I was told the phrase was also seldom used by men. Yeehaw. Barney gave me a friendly, manly pat on the back as I walked by him in the foyer. I hadn't taken a shower in days. I hoped I didn't smell like a homeless person. I surreptitiously sniffed toward my pits when I thought no one was looking. Yep, I smelled.

We used the nonemergency number to call the police. The closest police station was in Romney, West Virginia, a good ninety minutes from where we were.

A sleepy dispatcher answered the phone. He said there was nothing to be done about it until the morning.

There must have been fingerprints all over the car. I asked them to bring a fingerprint kit. I was bound and determined to catch the perpetrators. First, as a show of strength for my wife. Second, because how could I move my elderly parents here with the rampant crime? I had to clean this mess up before they got here. Third, because I was going to make the thieves take the car to the salvage yard. Good riddance.

When I was younger and before I met Anna, I stayed in D.C. for a few weeks with a friend. Brought my 1970 Camaro that I had painstakingly restored. It had fur on the ceiling and on the steering wheel. No one explained clearly enough that if you left anything of value in your car in D.C., it would get stolen. They just said lock your doors. So I did. The thieves broke the window and stole the four-foot speakers I had in the back. I didn't expect crime like that in West Virginia.

The dispatcher told me that heavy dew was predicted at dawn and that there would be no fingerprints left. So, send someone before dawn, right? But the car wasn't missing. The robbery attempt was unsuccessful. At best, we had a property damage claim. Low on the priority list for a station with a small budget. I was informed that a deputy would be out by noon the next day.

We thanked our lovely neighbors, Lydia and Barney, and went back to base camp. Anna dropped off a lovely fruit basket a few days later. They were our (and our parents') friends for life.

Turned out the neighbors who didn't answer the door were on vacation. They heard all about the hullabaloo when they came back. That's a word my grandfather loved. Didn't hear it so much nowadays.

We stopped by to introduce ourselves to the vacationing neighbors. They were elderly and a little hard of hearing. Said they probably wouldn't have heard us knocking and hollering even if they were home. We made sure to help them with firewood and odd jobs when they needed it.

We retrieved Anna's car before anyone plowed into it. I put her bumper in the van. I stood in the road waving a flashlight while we got the car turned around. Saw no one. I kept telling her to touch as little as possible to preserve fingerprints. Like that did any good.

As predicted by the dispatcher, heavy dew covered the hills when we woke up to morning birds singing at 6 a.m. The deputy arrived around 1 p.m. He half-heartedly dusted a few places on the outside of the car, which I think was solely to humor me. No need to dust anywhere inside because the car hadn't been unlocked by the would-be robbers.

He said they would investigate, but it was unlikely that they would find out who did this. Based on his walk-through of the crime scene, he determined that they must have attached a chain to Anna's bumper.

"I found pieces of chain on the road further down," said the deputy. "I don't think they would have been able to move a newer car that way if it had one of them new plastic bumpers."

Excellent deductive reasoning.

"You should park that big old van in front of the Cadillac so it won't happen again," he said.

What are the odds of that, right?

"Probably just some teenagers causing trouble," concluded the deputy. And off he went.

The driveway would be cleared and the gravel laid in about a week. There was no reason to drive Anna's car. So it just sat there by the road. Undisturbed by teenagers or anyone else.

I wanted to send a message to the locals that we were here permanently and that we would tolerate no more shenanigans. Like smoke signals, but with bullets. I ordered several cases of ammo for my shotgun. I had it delivered to the little town post office, where everyone in town went to pick up their mail. No driveway mailboxes for the county of less than 5,000 residents. I also ordered bright orange skeet.

We added shooting skeet to the list of fun activities Anna and I did in the woods as a newly married couple. We left the broken skeet pieces down near the road so it was clear what was going on here. That ought to do it.

Everyone in town was talking about the attempted car theft and the cases of ammo ordered by the Yankee newcomers, the postmaster informed us. Anyone driving by could see from the broken skeet that we were actively discharging firearms. We thought we would be left in peace.

The heavy equipment arrived. The driveway and the home site were cleared. No more walking the path through snake-infested briar brush. Temporary gravel was put down so we could move vehicles and equipment up the steep driveway.

I drove my van up to the site for the first time, lingering at the crest of the hill, imagining what everything would look like when we were all done. What a fantastic place this was going to be for my parents' retirement.

The tires of Anna's heavy car spun a little on the gravel on the way up the driveway. I yelled, "Don't lose speed. Keep a steady pressure on the gas pedal, or we'll have to take her back down the hill and start again."

My multitalented wife made it to the top on the first try and parked next to my van. She got out of her car and said, "I think something crawled up in my car and died while it was parked down there."

Great. "Probably in the engine. I'll take a look around," I said. I opened the hood and shined a flashlight all around. "I definitely smell it. It has to be here somewhere. I don't see anything in the engine. Maybe I can see better underneath."

I slid under the car with the flashlight, but no luck. "Maybe it's in the trunk," I said. I popped the trunk open, and a wave of decay hit me. In the trunk was a stained old tarp. I grabbed the edge of the tarp and tugged it back.

I yelled, "Holy Jehoshaphat!" No, I said "shit." And stumbled back from the car.

"Stay back, honey. You don't want to see this. I think it is a human skeleton," I said.

Talk about leaving a mark. But if you told my wife to do something, 99% of the time, she would do the opposite. I've used this knowledge to my advantage several times in our relationship, but I wasn't fast enough this time.

Side by side, we peered into the trunk. Several bones were visible. They were yellowed and caked with dirt. Couldn't even tell if the body was male or female.

I was waiting for hysterics. A scream. Crying. But no. Anna calmly said, "That was not in there when we got here."

Note to self, hiding skeletal remains was not on my wife's list of hidden talents. Thank Jehoshaphat. But she was calm in the face of death.

"Don't touch it," I said. After my miscalculation of her initial reaction, I thought I needed to state the obvious, just in case.

I slammed the trunk closed. We both jumped into the van because no one wanted to stay there alone with a dead body. Well, to be frank, the puppies did.

We drove down the road until we had cell service and called the police nonemergency number for the second time.

The sun was starting to set, and the same night dispatcher as the night of the attempted car robbery answered.

"There is a dead body in the trunk of our car," I said.

I could hear him sit up straighter in his chair and come to attention. "How do you know the body is dead?" he said.

"Um, the bones are yellowed and look old. There was no skin left on the bones that we could see," I said.

"Where's the car now?" he asked.

"It's at our construction site." I gave him directions.

"Where are you?"

"I'm about four miles away, holding my phone up above my head to grab a cell signal so I could call you."

"Do you know who the dead body is?"

"No."

"Did you kill the person?"

"No."

"Do you know who did?"

"No."

"Do you know how the dead body came to be in your car?"

"No."

"Don't touch anything. Return to the car and wait for the officer to arrive. He's on his way," said the dispatcher.

I was willing to bet they were going to bring a fingerprint kit this time.

About two hours later, the police officer arrived. Different than the one who investigated our almost car theft. He was the homicide detective.

He wrote down our names and told us to sit down and not to move until he came back to question us. He used the hand signal for stay. The puppies sat. Anna paced.

"Where is the car and the body?"

We both pointed to the rusting Cadillac.

"Did you touch anything?" he asked.

"I touched the corner of the tarp but nothing else," I said.

It was a long night. The police officer confirmed the body was, in fact, dead. Sorry, no zombies in this story. He radioed for the coroner to come. And yes, a full fingerprint team came over from Morgantown, along with crime scene techs. With generators. And lights. We probably had most of the West Virginia violent crimes team on our jobsite.

Anna built up the fire and started a pot of coffee. We put the dogs in the van to keep them out from underfoot. The police worked through the night. I was fascinated. I wanted to see more, but I was told to stay. With words. Not with hand signals that apparently had some flexible interpretation, at least to folks of the female persuasion.

The coroner was a beefy ex-football player doing his dead body job part-time. His other job was selling insurance. He confirmed that the body had been dead for several years. He could not determine the cause of death.

We were fingerprinted and questioned about where we were and what we knew, which wasn't much.

Not surprisingly, Anna's prints were found all over the car and the trunk, but not the body. My print was confirmed on the corner of the tarp but not otherwise inside the trunk. She and her parents had packed, and she had unpacked. Other prints from persons unknown were found in the trunk.

Anna's parents, Murray and Jane Schwartz, living in Michigan, were added to the growing list of suspects by the investigator.

As portly as the coroner was, the investigator, Chris Wilson, was tall and lean, almost skeletal. A man in his fifties with silver showing through his black hair, he seemed tired and pale, like he worked in a coal mine when not investigating homicides. There were plenty of coal mines in West Virginia. It was possible.

Anna told him that she removed everything she had packed from her trunk when she arrived at the jobsite and had not been in the trunk since then. The car had been sitting down at the side of the road for several days. She mentioned the attempted theft of the car. The investigator radioed headquarters to confirm the police report.

"Did you give access to your car to anyone?"

"No."

"Was your trunk locked?"

Anna and I looked at each other. We thought it was. But when I went to open the trunk, I just pressed the button where the key got inserted. I didn't need the key to open the trunk, which would have been the only way to do that in Anna's old car if the trunk had been locked. It didn't have a latch that would "pop" the trunk like the newer cars did. Maybe Anna had unlocked the trunk when she knew I was going to look for what we thought was going to be a dead animal in her car. She said she did not. So, the trunk must have been unlocked.

"I'm not sure," we replied in unison. Jinx.

Chris Wilson examined the trunk and lock carefully to see if there was any evidence that it had been tampered with. Nothing was visible.

He asked us all the same questions the dispatcher did: did we know who this was, did we kill this person, did we know who did, and why was the body in Anna's car? All great questions. But none that we could help him with. It was clear from his dour expression that he didn't believe us.

"Did you see anything out of the ordinary?"

"Just the attempted car theft."

"Anyone lurking around?"

"No."

By noon the next day, the police had taken Anna's car and the dead body away. Now I was going to have to go to Romney or Morgantown to pick up the car when they released it. (Not the dead body.) Maybe they wouldn't release the car. I wondered if we could just never pick it up. They could put the car in abandoned property. Fine with me.

We sat in stunned silence. No work was done on the house. We were too wired to sleep, although none of us had slept all night. How was I going to explain this to my parents?

The dogs were happy to have the hillside back to themselves.

The two goldens play-wrestled in the leaves not too far from us. Any lingering scent of a dead body, undetectable by us, only added to their enjoyment of the day.

"I thought the car was locked, but now I don't think so," said Anna. "It could have been anybody passing by. The guys delivering the construction equipment, fishermen, hunters, neighbors."

The Mafia. Drug cartels. Someone not from around here.

"Bet the gossip mill is going to be blowing up over this one," I said.

When the sun went down, the hillside was filled with the last fireflies of the season. We all went to sleep early. The list of things to do to prepare for move-in day just got a lot longer. Build a house. See that the perpetrators that placed the dead body in Anna's car were apprehended.

Chapter 2

HUBLER INTERNATIONAL CIRCUS

Said I: "my ambition is modest:
A clown in a circus I'd be,
and turn somersaults in the sawdust
With audience laughing at me."

Robert William Service
"My Future"

July 1981
Cumberland, MD

The young woman was a born entertainer. Ever since she was able to walk, she entertained people—singing, dancing, doing magic tricks, and performing in plays. The middle child, she was always the peacemaker, wanting everyone to like her. She didn't want to go to college. She thought that those four years would be a huge loss during her prime acting years. She wanted to be an entertainer. Like Lily Tomlin, Phyllis Diller, or Roseanne Barr.

In high school, she started working for an event company on the weekends, making balloons for fairs and festivals and dressed as a clown. She loved the anonymity the clown costume provided, pretending to be anyone she wanted to be. And she loved that the job made people laugh. She didn't want to be a serious actor and have to cry and get angry.

After graduating from high school in 1979, she decided she would join a circus. But each time she applied her applications were rejected. Not enough experience.

At the beginning of 1980, the University of Wisconsin-La Cross began offering evening continuing education clown classes. Dr. Richard Snowberg taught the class. He had been clowning since 1975, and his character was a famous "whiteface" clown called Snowflake. Her abilities increased exponentially in Dr. Snowberg's Clown Camp, as it was later called.

When the young woman sent out her applications to circuses in June 1980, she was accepted by the Hubler International Circus, which was based in Ohio. They toured the US, and she was excited to join the troupe. One of several clowns, she performed juggling and magic in the ring. Her stage name was Twinkles. The circus moved around by rail, and she loved the circus life. She would watch the other performers rehearse, constantly learning new tricks and nuances for her show.

In July 1981, she had been with Hubler for about a year. That month, they were scheduled to perform in Cumberland.

The first night, the show was sold out. One of her magic tricks, which involved pulling a colorful scarf out of someone's ear, was a huge crowd-pleaser, so she had been moved to the front of the ring, closest to the audience.

In the front row sat a big, burly mountain man with a full black beard. Beside him sat two boys, maybe eight or nine years old. The boys were mesmerized by the performance.

She chose the man for her scarf-out-of-the-ear trick. When she leaned over the rail, the little boys' eyes grew wide. The man was a good sport as she removed the scarf from the man's ear, fluttering it over her head.

At the end of the trick, she spun around to return to her mark and continue her show, but as she did, the scarf fluttered down and caught on a splinter on the railing of the risers. It ripped as she pulled it toward her. No big deal. No one noticed, and she didn't need the scarf in any of her other tricks.

The next day, there was no matinee scheduled. She couldn't use the ripped scarf for the evening show. No one had an extra one that they were not using in their own performances.

She could either exclude the trick for the night or go into town to see if she could find a replacement scarf. The weather was beautiful. The sky had fluffy white clouds floating across it. She decided to walk into town.

On the main street, she found a G.C. Murphy, a five-and-dime store. She bought a silky red scarf. Delighted with her purchase, she nearly skipped down the street. But while she was in the store, a storm had blown in over the mountains, and fat raindrops started to fall.

She ducked into a drug store with an ice cream counter while she waited for the rain to pass. Inside, other people surprised by the summer rain had the same idea. One of them was the man from her performance the night before.

"I pulled a scarf from your ear last night," she said to the man.

"Well, now, I didn't recognize you without your costume and makeup on," said the man. "Weren't callin' for no rain today. Bit of a surprise."

"Yes," she said. "I didn't even carry an umbrella."

"I was thinking of making a run for it to my truck," the man said. "Can I give you a lift back to the circus?"

"No, I'm fine. I'll just wait it out," she said. "But thank you."

"Are you sure?" said the man. "It doesn't look like it's going to let up anytime soon. I'd be happy to drop you off. It's on the way back home."

In the last year, the young woman had performed in more than fifty cities, small and large. Everyone welcomed the circus and was always friendly and helpful. When you drew an audience member into your show, you felt like you knew them.

"Well, if it is no trouble . . ." she said.

They left the drugstore and dashed to the man's truck parked several feet from the entrance. She got in on the passenger side and set her shopping bag at her feet.

As they pulled away from the curb, the man asked, "Been doin' some shopping?"

"I needed a new scarf for the show tonight," she said and slipped the scarf partway out of the bag to show him.

"My boys loved your trick last night," said the man. "I don't want to put you out none, but they'd love to see some more. We can't get over to the show tonight, but you mind if we swing by the house, and you could do a couple tricks for 'em?"

She looked at her watch and saw that she still had several hours before call time.

"Okay, maybe I can teach them a couple of easy ones that they can do," she said. She was inspired by Dr. Snowberg and wanted to give back by teaching others the craft.

They drove through the country and turned down a long dirt driveway through a forest. At the end of the drive was a cabin with five steps leading up to the door. The man honked his horn as he pulled up to the front.

"Boys, have I got a surprise for you," said the man. "Get over here quick."

The boys came down the steps two at a time. The young woman got out of the truck and said, "Your dad asked me to teach you a couple of magic tricks. I'm Twinkles, the clown that you saw last night at the circus."

"Wow, that's cool!" said one of the boys. "Can you make my brother disappear?" He pushed the younger boy playfully.

She didn't have any of her props with her, so she used a stone and made it disappear in her hand. She spent several minutes teaching the boys, who were fast learners.

As her hand moved, the charm bracelet her parents had given her as a birthday present tinkled. The younger boy held her hand, turning it so he could look at the little charms.

She also did the scarf trick with her new scarf, using the younger boy as her assistant.

"OK, boys, we've got to get the lady back to the circus now. Go on in and help your Ma," said the man.

Twinkles the Clown and the man got back in the truck,

and the man drove down the driveway heading for the road. He stopped about halfway down the drive out of sight of the house.

"I saw a nail in the drive," said the man. "Wanted to pick it up before the missus or I run it over and get a flat. Must of fell out of my truck bed."

Before she could even comment, the man exited the truck. She looked in the passenger side mirror and saw the man walk behind the truck. All of a sudden, her door was yanked open. The man pulled her out of the truck and threw her to the ground. Something was wrapped around her throat so tight she couldn't take a breath to scream. She lost consciousness in seconds. Twinkles the Clown died there in the driveway.

During the evening call at the circus, the young woman's boss, a clown named Happy, noticed she was missing. He asked her co-workers if they knew where she was. One of them told him she had gone into town to buy a scarf. No one had seen her since.

He reorganized the performance schedule. He instructed a couple of the animal caretakers to search the camp for her. When the evening show ended and the woman was still not located, he called the police.

The police visited several of the stores in town that carried scarves. A shop clerk at Murphy's remembered her. After that, there was no trace of her.

Happy notified George Hubler, the big man himself, of her disappearance. People were known to run away to the circus, but also to run away from the circus. Mr. Hubler called the young woman's parents and told them she was missing. They arrived from Wisconsin the next day. Flyers were posted; people were interviewed.

The case was relegated to the cold case files after a few years. The young woman's parents could not fathom that their bright, effervescent daughter was gone. She wanted to be a clown so badly they could not believe that she would just leave. She was always so responsible.

Chapter 3

FOUNDATION

Foundation: the lowest load-bearing part of a building, typically at or below ground level. Offers support to and anchors the structure by transmitting the load to the ground.

A person was accused of burying someone in cement. But there was no concrete evidence.

Beginning of October 1994

Not to toot my own horn, but I was multitalented when it came to construction. Carpentry, plumbing, electrical, heating, and air conditioning. I was planning to do all of that work on my parents' house myself, with the help of some family members. And a buddy of mine would come down when the logs arrived. But I wanted a professional to lay the block basement and foundation so the base layer of the house would be done right.

We hired Sonny Atherton, a guy based in Paw Paw, West Virginia. With a couple hundred residents, the town was absolutely bustling compared to our local post office and country store. It was located not far from the other side of the trestle bridge where the train crossed the river. We could see the bridge off in the distance.

I have no idea how we found Sonny, but there weren't that many options at the time. He had a deep West Virginia accent that was sometimes hard to understand. He was always chewing tobacco. Sonny had a sunny disposition and was easy to work with.

He brought in a couple of friends, and they had the block installed in about a week.

Because the house was built into the hill, the garage was in the basement. You would enter the garage from the left side of the house. If you walked up to the front door, it was at ground level. Everything below ground was concrete block. The plans called for three bedrooms and 2.5 baths with a loft area. We were planning to combine the two bedrooms upstairs into a second master for visitors.

To be clear, "just on the other side of the trestle bridge" was literal, not a euphemism. Or sarcasm. Literally, Paw Paw was just a couple of miles away if you used the train tracks to cross the river. Otherwise, it was a forty-minute drive on the roads.

Sonny said all the locals drove over on the tracks. The train crossed only twice per day, and they all knew the schedule. He said we should try it sometime.

Funny name for a town, Paw Paw. In Native American, it was a fruit resembling papaya that grew abundantly in that region of West Virginia. A Portuguese explorer saw the Native Americans eating the fruit. When he said "papaya," the Native Americans understood "paw paw." Made sense to me.

Ironically, there's a town named Paw Paw in Michigan, too. It was named after the nearby Paw Paw River, which was, in turn, named after that same fruit.

I had also heard "paw paw" used as a term of endearment for "grandfather." As you might imagine, we got a lot of West Virginia inbreeding jokes from our friends in Michigan before we came down. I chuckled to myself that Sonny was from Paw Paw. I thought, "*Let me introduce you to my father, who is my cousin.*" Based on the many wonderful people we met in West Virginia, I could tell you those stories were highly exaggerated.

One day when we had completed all of our post-project activities (pork and beans, throw the ball, skeet shooting), we crossed the trestle bridge on the train tracks over to Paw Paw. Afterward, I thought Sonny was yanking our chain.

The tracks were laid on two twelve-inch-wide wooden boards, with nothing but a hundred feet of air down to the river below. It took us nearly an hour to drive cautiously across the bridge. I could have walked across faster. Well, or scooted across on my butt.

We never told Sonny we drove across on the tracks, and

we would never do it again. But it was something to cross off your bucket list that you never even knew was on your bucket list. Terrifying and exhilarating all at the same time. Stupid foreigners. I hear my mother's voice in the back of my head; something she probably said to me many, many times: "Just because everyone else is jumping off a cliff doesn't mean you have to." In my defense, I didn't think it was going to be cliff-diving.

While the block foundation was going up, my parents, Yvonne and Nick Bradley, came down from Michigan for their first site visit since we broke ground.

They stayed in a no-frills Best Western in Cumberland, Maryland, about thirty minutes away. I took a gloriously long hot shower in their room.

I'd been bathing in the river, taking my soap and a towel and wading into the middle of the river. There was a big, flat stone to sit on that was submerged just deep enough when the river was running normally. The Z goldens would stand on the bank of the river, whining and crying, and pacing back and forth. They were golden retrievers. They liked water. I have seen them in the river. They would sometimes cross to the huge pasture on the other side of the river, following a deer. Something in their doggie code prohibited them from joining me in the river while I was washing up. Maybe they were afraid I would soap them up too? No dog wants to smell like Irish Spring.

The plunge into the river was harder as it got colder. I was the one who insisted we rough it. Anna never complained. One more bucket list thing. Been there, done that. Never again.

Sonny was there when my parents visited the site and loved "Momma," as he called her. Yvonne was charmed.

"I'm a little worried about how steep the driveway is," Yvonne said to Sonny. "How will we get our car up?" They had a Lincoln Town Car, almost as big as Anna's Cadillac, minus the fins.

Sonny said, "Momma, you don't have to worry none. Once we get the shell on there, you won't have any problem."

Yvonne turned to me with absolute wonder shining in her eyes and said, "You didn't tell me you were putting seashells on the driveway."

Sonny looked at me in confusion. "No, ma'am, *shell*," he said again.

I know how much she would LOVE seashells, but it wasn't in the budget. With Sonny's deep West Virginia accent, he spoke the word shale without any of the "ay" us Northerners expected, so the word did sound like "shell". I hated to disappoint her, but I said, "Mom, your driveway is going to be shale."

"Oh," she said and giggled.

Sonny said, "Yes'm, *shell*."

My mother told that story many times, and we did end up putting shells in the concrete between her paving stones leading up to the front door as an inside joke, which we all loved.

Forensics came back with a report on the dead body found in Anna's car. The body had been dead over ten years. Okay, so not from an ancient Indian burial ground. The body was a young female. No ID. No cause of death could be determined. Soil testing indicated the body had been buried somewhere in the county.

Because none of us were ever in West Virginia before a

few weeks ago, we were off the murder suspect list; if it was a murder. We still might be on the list of suspects for tampering with a body. I guessed the police thought we uncovered it while digging the house site and stashed it in the car for safekeeping, then called the police when it started to smell.

One day, I stopped by the post office in town to pick up mail. The "town" consisted of the tiniest post office I have ever seen and a country store that had an inventory of about a hundred items. They had pork and beans and plenty of nails. I was all set. The post office was alongside the railroad tracks that ran over the trestle bridge to Paw Paw with the train that passed through twice a day. The post office was brick, and inside was a counter with a pickup window and a small 10 x 15-foot entryway. The PO boxes were behind the counter. The only way to get your mail was to be there when the postmaster was there. Although the hours were posted, he might be there or he might not, just depending. He had no backup. And he did not give the impression the post office was his priority. I think he had about six kids.

Our neighbor, Curtis, was in the post office entry. When I said hello, he gave no indication that he recognized me from the day in the woods with the trencher. I got a polite nod. Okay, that was fine. I smiled and walked up to the window.

The postmaster was a young guy in his thirties. He lived within walking distance of the post office. His house and a few other trailers rounded out the town.

"Heard you folks had some trouble up your way," he said. "They found out who that girl was?"

"Not that I am aware. How are the kids?" I asked, trying to change the subject. Although I fully expected Curtis to join in the conversation, he turned on his heel and walked out the door.

"Terrible thing," said the postmaster, shaking his head. "Kids are great. But I worry about 'em. Our little town has become quite the high-crime area."

My antenna went up. "Why? Did something else happen?"

"Potter's prize bull was stolen out his field t'other day. Police went and found it hidden in someone's basement. Poor guy that owned the house, he and the missus dint know it was there 'til it started to smell. Turns out, some kin done stole it," he said. "Fact, I think they related in some way to Curtis that just left."

No wonder he didn't want to hang around and tell stories with the postmaster. That would have been awkward. I wanted to know more.

"Isn't cattle rustling a felony in West Virginia?" I asked. I was pretty sure it was in Texas. Not so sure about West Virginia.

I also wanted to know how they could have gotten the bull down the stairs into the basement. How did they feed it? How did they get it back up the stairs? Would they be charged with animal cruelty? How would you get the smell of cow manure out of the basement? I kept all of these questions to myself.

With no TV, I could mull over these challenges that evening while eating hotdogs and baked beans over the fire.

It reminded me of a story I read about where a neighbor snuck onto the adjacent farm and stole semen from the prize bull. Fertilization of a cow with a dose of semen brought in a fee of hundreds of thousands of dollars a pop. Little cows started popping up in the neighbor's field that looked just like the farmer's prize bull, but no fertilization was authorized or paid for. The owner of the prize bull sued.

This, admittedly, had different logistical problems than the two West Virginia boys who probably didn't want to give a hand job to the bull, they just stole the whole thing. I could just imagine the conversation. I named the guys Darryl and Other Brother Darryl after an old *Bob Newhart Show* episode.

Darryl: "Come on, man, all you got to do is stroke it for a few minutes and catch the stuff in this here pot."

Other Brother Darryl: "I'm not stroking no bull's thing or watching him jizz into a pot."

Darryl: "Well then, what do you think we should do?"

Other Brother Darryl: "Let's take him to uncle's house and hide him in the basement 'til we can stud him out. Maybe our sister, who is our aunt, would want to give the big guy a tug job."

Right, made a lot of sense. Now I knew why the police thought we moved the body, stashed it in the trunk, then called them. They dealt with criminals who would rather take the whole bull than yank out the semen.

At the post office in West Virginia, the postmaster said, "I ain't sure, but they's been arrested and sittin' in jail right now. Them boys have been nothing but trouble since they started runnin' by theyselves."

"What other kind of trouble?" I asked.

Just teenage stuff," he said. "Breakin' windows, petty theft, drinkin', shootin' road signs, that kinda thing. They's well known to local law enforcement."

I bet that police officer who investigated the almost-theft of Anna's car knew exactly who tried to take it. Didn't need any fingerprint kit to solve that crime.

"So glad Mr. Potter got his bull back safe and sound. See you soon!"

I walked out the door to my van. I saw Curtis still sitting in his truck in the gravel lot, reading his mail.

While Sonny from Paw Paw was working on the foundation, we prepared to pull the electrical wire through the conduit in the trench that Anna and I dug. We had threaded it with rope before we buried it so we could pull the wire when we were ready for the hookup. The rope was tied to a stake in the ground at each end.

I put a temporary electrical panel on a pole up near the house site. I was looking forward to electricity in the evening.

I walked over to the end of the conduit closest to the house, the dogs bouncing around my feet. Oh yeah, Dad was going for a walk. There was no rope. I looked all around. Stake in the ground. No rope.

I jogged back to the house. Found Anna. She didn't touch the rope. The men on Sonny's crew said they didn't even know where the electrical conduit was.

Maybe the rope just slipped down into the pipe and I could fish it out. Before doing that, I wanted to make sure that it was anchored on the other end.

The frolicking puppies and I walked to the back of the twenty-acre lot. Oh boy. With deer. And rabbits. And squirrels. And snakes. Dog heaven.

I inspected the stake on that end. No rope. What the hell? This was impossible.

I looked down into the pipe. I shined a flashlight a few

feet into the pipe before it made the turn. No rope.

Someone must have tampered with it. And it was impossible to put the rope back through without digging the whole thing up again.

The magnitude of this vandalism settled in. I was getting the feeling that someone didn't want us here. Could it be something more than locals who were opposed to the new development? Or just some neighborhood kids playing a prank with no appreciation for the damage they caused?

Darryl: "Hey, look at this here rope. Wonder what it's for?"

Other Brother Darryl: "I dunno, but let's cut it off to mess with whoever put it here."

To cut it off at both ends would take a vandal smarter and more premeditated than my imaginary Darryls. I whistled for the dogs, and we walked dejectedly back to camp.

Nothing to be done about it that day. We'd need to rent the trencher again, if it was even available, and wait days for it to be delivered. One upside: maybe I'd get the chance to operate it myself? Probably not. Anna would get to have all the fun again.

After dinner, I was sitting by the fire, thinking about this problem we now faced. In my younger years, I was a volunteer firefighter. Applying some engineering logic, I wondered if a firehose could force enough water through the pipe. Worth exploring.

In the morning, I went to the fire department. I figured showing up in person would be better than talking on the phone, which we didn't have easy access to, anyway. I walked into a new building with two gleaming fire trucks sitting in the bay.

John, an on-call volunteer, was sitting behind a table. I explained my problem.

"Sorry to hear about your troubles," said John. "Afraid that's not a great welcome to the neighborhood. Let me go get the captain. He's out back."

John and Captain Adkins returned shortly. "Let's hear this crazy idea you have," said Captain Adkins.

"What if you brought out a pump truck and put a firehose nozzle into the conduit? Then we tie a rope to the end of a light ball. Do you think the water pressure from the hose could push the ball some 500 feet or so to rethread the pipe?" I asked.

John and Captain Adkins were quiet for a few minutes while they contemplated this. "Son," said Captain Adkins, "I think that could work. We'd certainly be willing to try it for a fellow firefighter."

"I'll be happy to make a donation to the station," I said.

"No need," said Captain Adkins. "Professional courtesy. Maybe if you stick around, you would consider joining the team. We could use your ingenuity."

The next day, the entire crew of eight showed up on two engine trucks. No one wanted to miss out on this experiment. They came with sirens and lights blaring, so everyone for miles would know. No pressure. Including our possible skeleton mover? Maybe.

Many of the neighbors along the route came to watch like it was a sporting event. Or a burning building. People introduced themselves to us. If they were Mafia, they were hiding in plain sight.

Cherry, who lived further down the road, knew many of the firefighters personally. She arrived with donuts and coffee.

And a smile. And sparkles.

Cherry was an exotic dancer. She had bright red hair. She told me that was why her mother named her Cherry. Talk about predisposing your child's career choices. Cherry danced at one of the two clubs in the county.

One, called The Dover, was family owned. All of the women in the family danced. I kid you not. Mother, daughters, cousins. Even Mee Maw had been known on occasion to get on the stage. Although since Paw Paw passed (sorry, I couldn't resist), most of her work was done behind the scenes.

Cherry danced at the other club, called the Scruze Club. Cherry was also the one who mansplained "bless your heart" to me.

I admit that while we were building the house, there were a couple times when Anna went home to visit her parents and I would go to see Cherry dance at Scruze. She was a great dancer. Anna said it would be fine if I went. Not sure if she meant it, but she knew who she was marrying. During our time in West Virginia, Anna and Cherry became good friends. I knew she had Cherry spy on me. So, I behaved myself in a manner befitting an audience member in an exotic dancing establishment who knew their wife was spying on them.

Also in attendance for the firefighter feat of nature was Otto Rutherford. He lived in the house closest to our site, about a mile away. Otto retired from the FBI several years ago. He was an "analyst." In spook speak, I thought that could mean anything from a "super spy" to an accountant crunching numbers at a desk.

He bought the original 1860s historic homestead on the property, which was subdivided into ten- to twenty-acre lots in the development. He wasn't the original owner, though.

The property had already been subdivided and sold. The family made beaucoup bucks and got the hell out of West Virginia. The grass was always greener.

He and his wife moved out of D.C. to live a quiet, crime-free life in the mountains of West Virginia. This was the first time we met.

Sonny and his crew didn't want to miss the action, either. They all seemed to know Cherry, too. They stood around watching. No work on the block foundation got done. Darryl and Other Brother Darryl didn't appear to be in attendance.

I was ready with several types of light balls acquired in Cumberland the night before, not at the local place next to our post office. I got a whiffle ball, a practice golf ball with holes, a rubber dog toy with holes, and strong nylon climbing rope.

After much discussion among the crew about which ball to try first, we settled on the whiffle ball. We tied the rope with the ball to the stake and dropped the ball and rope down into the conduit.

With everything set up at the end of the conduit closest to the house, Captain Adkins, a couple of other firefighters, and I set off for the other end of the conduit. Captain Adkins communicated with his crew via walkie-talkie.

"John, light her up," said Captain Adkins.

"Yes, sir. System's pressurized. Water coming your way," said John.

We stood back, waiting for the water to travel hundreds of feet to our end of the conduit. I held my breath.

"John, we have water exiting the pipe but no ball and no rope. Shut off the pressure," said the captain.

"Roger that," said John.

"Don't worry," said the captain. "Now we know the water

pressure should be adequate. We just need a heavier ball. See if you can pull the rope back out. Use the heavier rubber dog ball and tie it to the rope. Let's see if that'll work," said the captain. "If you can't pull it out, use a new rope and leave the old one in there."

John and a couple of the other firefighters were able to pull the whiffle ball and rope back out. Pulling against the water inside the pipe required some strength.

A long stream of water exited the pipe at our end, forced out by the new water John was adding on his end. Then the dog ball attached to the rope shot out of the pipe, rope attached.

"Success," cried the captain. He turned to me and shook my hand. "Brilliant, young man."

I wanted to hug him, but he didn't seem like the hugging type. I did a fist pump in the air instead. "Thank you, Captain, this has been an enormous help. You have no idea," I said.

"Well, young man, we're used to rescuing people in all kinds of situations. This was a first for us, but it was great fun. Do stop by the station if you decide to stay in the area," he said.

You could hear cheers from the onlookers floating over the hill when John announced the success. We donated $500 to the firehouse, despite the captain's objections. It would have cost us that to rent the trencher, not including the time we would have lost to dig up the pipe.

I wanted to mingle with some of the neighbors like Cherry, but I still had some work to do. I had to dig a small hole to puncture the pipe so the water would drain out, then seal it back up, then pull the electrical wire and get it hooked up and locked down tight so this couldn't happen again.

For a minute, I fantasized about leaving a low-voltage wire exposed. That might deter any further vandalism. *ZZZT.*

But then I worried about what would happen if a deer touched it. Or a bear. So I didn't.

I made a mental note to call the police detective tomorrow to find out what was happening with the investigation of the dead body from Anna's trunk.

The firemen packed up their gear and headed out. Onlookers took the leftover donuts with them as they left. A great day was had by all. And I felt like a hero. Just a little bit. Anna did a great job of stroking my ego after dinner.

I wondered if I should write this up as a case study for Fire Fighter Magazine. You never know. Some other poor bastard might encounter people trying to run him out of town by vandalizing his underground electrical conduit. It could happen.

Chapter 4

SUBFLOOR

Subfloor: an important base for the flooring system.
Provides a structurally sound flat surface
for the finished floor.

Why are men like finished hardwood flooring?
Lay one right the first time, and you can
walk all over it the rest of your life.

End of October 1994

Sonny and his crew wrapped up the block work. I was sad to see them go. They had been great company and an excellent source for jobsite pranks and jokes, for which I was infamous. They gave as good as they got. They were coming back to do the fireplace and the stone facing on the foundation in a few months. I looked forward to that. And my next visit to Scruze.

I called Detective Wilson to get an update on the case. Among ourselves, we were calling the body "Sally," after the character in the movie *Nightmare Before Christmas*, which was released the year before, that Anna and I saw together.

Their investigation was at a dead end. They had no leads, no further information. Blah blah blah. Don't call us, we'll call you.

I could tell by his voice that he still suspected we had something to do with this. Or maybe he just resented us for the extra workload. Yeah, couldn't we have just taken care of the problem ourselves and not involved the police? If you were from West Virginia, you would have just taken care of it yourself. Stupid foreigners.

For the I don't know how many times, I asked myself how I was going to explain this to my parents.

When I met our neighbor, Otto Rutherford, he said we should stop by any time. Now, I knew that people said that but didn't really mean it. But, since I had no cell service, it wasn't like I could have called him to ask him if now was a good time.

On a Sunday afternoon when I felt like I needed a break, I jumped in the van and drove the mile over to his house. I put on my best flannel shirt. I grabbed a six-pack of beer. It was cold because I plugged a min-fridge into the temporary electrical panel. Ah, electricity. That was another thing I missed.

I left Anna snuggled up in the tent that we had moved into the basement of the house, partially covered with subflooring. She was reading a book and serving as a puppy chew toy. What a woman.

Otto's house was a stately country estate. I'd say about 4,000 square feet, well preserved and restored. I knew that since he bought the place, he added a swimming pool. And a tennis court. And a driving range. And a helicopter pad.

I walked up to the columned porch and rang the doorbell. I wondered if he would answer the door packing heat. Nah, he probably had some fancy security system and knew who it was before he answered.

Otto was in his late sixties, average height, with a full head of gray hair. He wore "professor" glasses, as Anna called them. He answered the door wearing corduroy pants and a button cable knit sweater. An Oxford shirt with no tie. He was spry with intelligent eyes and full of energy.

I handed him the six-pack and followed him through to a glass-enclosed back porch. The room was filled with comfortable rattan furniture overlooking the pool and tennis court. He popped two beers, one for me, then one for himself. He settled in a chair, put his leather-slippered feet on an ottoman, and said, "How is the construction coming?"

"Great," I said. "We're still more or less on schedule. The block foundation's finished, and we're working on building the subfloor. Should be done in a few days. Then we'll be dry and cozy in the basement while we finish the rest of the house. And I can heat the basement with portable propane heaters."

Heaven. "Your house is beautiful. When did you move in?"

"We found it a couple of years ago. Moved out here from D.C."

"That's a big change," I said.

"It was time," Otto said. "The city just kept getting more and more crowded, and crime was always increasing. When I retired from the FBI, I wanted a simple, stress-free life. I love it here. I heard about the trouble up at your place with the body in your wife's car. Have the police made any progress in the investigation?"

"Unfortunately, no. No leads. No ID. And not too motivated to solve the case of a decades-old body turning up all of a sudden. I have to say, I'm going to worry about my parents being here if this doesn't get solved," I said.

I know what you are thinking: why didn't they just do a DNA analysis? In 1994, DNA was still extremely controversial. In 1987, a rapist in Florida named Tommie Lee Andrews was the first person in the US to be convicted of a crime using DNA evidence. And DNA was used in the conviction of the South Side Strangler in Virginia in 1988. In West Virginia in 1994, they were not using DNA to identify bodies. Even if they had DNA from the long-buried bones, there were no databases to compare it to.

I hesitated, not knowing whether Otto could somehow be involved in the Sally case. Moving the body off his property. Exigent circumstances. Had to stash it in Anna's car? I weighed the odds. Unlikely.

"Do you have any suggestions on what we could do to aid in the investigation?" I asked.

"Honestly," Otto said, "I have a vested interest in the outcome of the investigation. Such a horrible thing so close to my new residence. I want answers too. I still have some resources at the FBI. Let me see what I can do."

"That would be wonderful," I said. *Or you could be working to cover up the crime.* "Do you think that the body might've been buried somewhere in the subdivision? Maybe whoever put it here got nervous with all the building going on."

"That's one possibility," he said. "Let me see if I can get a copy of the autopsy report. I think they found that the soil on the skeleton was similar to the soil here. I'll confirm, and if so, then maybe we should do an informal search of the neighborhood. See if we can find any disturbed ground where the body may have been buried. Maybe some of the neighbors would help."

"But what if it's one of the neighbors that put the body in Anna's car?" I asked.

"There are a couple of folks I trust," said Otto.

Please say Cherry, please say Cherry.

"Do you know Rob Livingston over in the octagonal-shaped house toward the end of the road?" he asked.

I had marveled at the complexity of the house. And wondered why anyone would want eight-sided walls instead of just four.

"No, I don't think I've met him," I said. "But I have seen his house from the outside. It looks cool."

"He's ex-CIA, and I know he shares my interest in solving this," said Otto.

Or he needed a place to stash dead Russian spies and hid them out here or was moving them out here. I could be somewhat of a pessimist.

"Let's get the results of that autopsy and schedule something if the data is positive. I'll host a search party," said Otto.

Oh, the fun you could have in West Virginia.

Otto walked me to the door and asked, "By any chance, do you play tennis?"

I said, "I used to play all the time with my parents. Haven't played in a while so I'm probably rusty, but I'd love to play sometime."

I wished him a good evening, and he seemed happy. A new case and possible tennis partner. I wanted to see a helicopter land on that helipad.

⚒

The logs for the log home were scheduled to be delivered in a couple of days. Anna and I applied ourselves to finishing the subfloor. After my morning coffee, I stood watching the rising sun burn off the low-lying fog over the river.

I put on my toolbelt to complete the last of the subfloor. Missing from my belt were my hammer, a small pry bar, and a couple of screwdrivers. Upon reflection, I'd been "losing" a lot of tools recently. I finally broke down and went to the hardware store and bought several hammers.

It wasn't unusual for tools to go missing on a site. But an inordinate number of tools had disappeared lately.

My first suspects were the vandals who sabotaged our electric setup. Another attempt to drive us out by stealing my tools. And drive me crazy. But they would have had to come right onto the jobsite to do this. Hard to do that unnoticed at this point.

Second suspects, the Brothers Darryl. "Hey, let's go take some of that guy's hammers. That'll make him give up building and leave." No, probably not.

I asked Anna.

"No, haven't seen them. You leave your stuff all over. It's no wonder you can't find anything."

Oh boy, she sounded just like my mother. I checked the basement and outside around the house. No missing tools. Another mystery to solve.

Later that day, Otto came walking up the driveway. He had a walking stick and was wearing a barn coat. "I hope you don't mind me stopping by," said Otto.

Still no phone, so you couldn't call. It was not like we were going anywhere or doing anything other than building. I hoped he brought beer. I wondered if he would volunteer the use of his shower.

"I got a copy of that autopsy report. The soil appears to be local to the area," Otto said.

Anna said, "It would be great to find out what happened to Sally."

"Sally?" Otto asked.

"Oh, sorry," Anna said. "We've been calling her Sally after the character in the movie *Nightmare Before Christmas*."

"Haven't seen it," said Otto, "but Sally is as good a name as any until we find out her real name."

"Do you think we will?" asked Anna.

"I truly hope so," he said. "I would hate to think of her parents out there wondering what happened to their daughter and all the years of not knowing. As we talked about the other day, I'm going to organize an informal search of the properties here in the subdivision."

"Just tell us when and where, and we'll be there," I said.

"The weather looks good for tomorrow. Do you think you could make that work?" Otto asked.

"Sure. I'll wrap up this subfloor today, and then we're

just waiting on the logs to be delivered at the end of the week. We'll bring the goldens. Train them to search," I said. Or they'll just be some light entertainment and comfort for what could be a gruesome task.

Otto said, "Let's gather at my house around 9 a.m. tomorrow. I can introduce you to some of the other neighbors. We can set up some search grids and see what we find."

Snakes, I was thinking.

The next morning, Anna, the two goldens, and I arrived at Otto's house just before 9 a.m. Several people were milling about. It looked like people assembled for a fox hunt. Two tables were set outside, one with pastries, finger foods, and coffee. The other had a large map of the area.

Otto introduced us to Rob Livingston. Now, *he* looked like the typical mountain man. Heavy set, heavily bearded. He was wearing rubber waders. I bet he was afraid of snakes, too. He had a shoulder holster with a pistol in view. Probably for the bears. Did I feel safer? I wasn't sure. I wondered if I should go back and get my shotgun.

Sadly, Cherry was not among the people assembled.

Otto asked everyone to gather around the table with the map. There were nine people total, including Anna, Otto, and me. Zeus and Zoey were off looking for rabbits, and I watched them zip back and forth, investigating all the new scents.

Otto suggested we split up into four groups. Each group was assigned to search a quarter of the subdivision. We had the east section, including the property where we were building my parents' house. Otto was leading the group for the north section. Rob, the south section. He handed one person in each group a walkie-talkie. Now this was some high tech.

"Check in if you find anything of interest," said Otto. "If not, at least every hour. Let's meet back here around noon for lunch. Sandwiches are being brought over. Whatever we don't finish in the morning, we should be able to get done by three. Please remember, if you do find something, do not touch it or trample the ground around it. I will call the police if there is something out there. Safe searching."

And we were off. I felt like I was in a dream. I was in West Virginia. Searching for a burial site where a dead body was disturbed. When I signed on for this family adventure of a lifetime, I could not have predicted this.

I called the dogs. Anna and I headed back to the building site. We started there, moving further east until the subdivision edge. Then we would head back west toward Otto's house. We had about sixty acres to cover, three of the twenty lots in the subdivision.

The sun was shining through the trees that had all lost their leaves already. A slight wind was blowing, but not too cold. Anna picked up a long stick. She was beating the brush ahead of her as she walked. Smart woman. I walked behind her. Great view. No snakes.

The walkie-talkie crackled to life. My heart skipped a beat. Had someone found something already?

Otto's voice: "System check on the walkie-talkies. All groups, please confirm."

"Sam here, confirmed," I said. The other groups did likewise.

We were a few hundred yards to the east of the house site. I saw a small mound not natural in the landscape. Maybe a pile of brush or a fallen tree? I veered off to investigate, Zoey and Zeus in hot pursuit.

They passed me and sat down in front of the pile. Odd, I thought. As I got closer, they lay down, side by side. Even odder. I asked, "What is it, guys?" as I walked closer. Their tails thumped in unison. OK, not danger.

The pile was not brush or a fallen tree or snakes. It was a crapload of my tools. My little golden puppy thieves had been stealing my tools and stockpiling them on this hidey pile. Oh, you bad puppies. Oh, you funny puppies. It was so ridiculous I burst out laughing. Just golden antics. Not the Mafia, not the Darryls.

All the groups checked in on the walkie-talkies every hour. We reached the easternmost edge of the subdivision and started back. It was almost noon, so we turned around and headed to Otto's house.

He did indeed have a spread of sandwiches to feed the hungry hordes. It was catered by none other than Scruze. And delivered by you know who, Cherry. Otto, my man, I would marry you in a heartbeat if it wasn't for Anna. And if I played for the other team.

The groups returned and settled around the pool to eat. The dogs raced across the fields looking for rabbits. I hoped tool acquisition was just a phase that they grew out of. Otherwise, I was going to need to get more duplicates. At least now I knew where to go if I needed something.

While we were eating, Zeus came running over with what looked like a stick in his mouth. He settled at my feet and chewed on it. Zoey was bouncing around him because she didn't have a stick. I found one and gave it to her so she would chill while we ate.

Otto came over and sat down next to us. He said, "The dogs must be great company for you."

"Hmm," I said. And a recent source of tool depletion.

"What you got there, boy? Did you find a stick?" Otto said to Zeus. He reached over to scratch Zeus behind the ears. Otto looked closer and said, "I don't think that's a stick. It looks like a bone."

"Probably a deer bone," I said. "He finds them all the time and brings them to us."

Otto picked up a stick and gave it to Zeus and then took the bone away from him. He wrapped his hand in a napkin before he touched the bone. Now Zeus may still have been a puppy, but he didn't just fall off the turnip truck. He knew the difference between a bone and a stick, and he was not happy. But I raised him right – he was polite. He accepted the stick with sad eyes and relinquished his prize.

Zoey gave Zeus a smart-ass eye roll that meant, "I knew you couldn't keep control of that, dumbass."

Otto carried the bone over to the table with the map. Rob came over to inspect. After some discussion, it was not clear to them whether this was an animal bone or a human bone. Then a discussion ensued about whether to call the police. And how stupid some of us would feel if it was a deer bone. Not me. Given everything that had happened, I'd call the police. They already thought I was an idiot.

We would also have to explain our little merry band of searchers. One of the other searchers approached us, a colleague of Otto's who was still with the FBI. He offered to take the bone to have it analyzed at the FBI lab that afternoon. If it was human, they would alert the police. If not, the bone would be returned to its finder, Zeus. His ears perked up. His tail wagged. *Don't tease me*, his eyes said.

Rather than finish the search, we postponed to wait for the bone analysis. The police would want to do a formal search if this bone was human. Could we be dealing with a second dead body in the wilds of West Virginia?

Sirens were echoing off the mountains in our little slice of heaven at 10 a.m. the next morning. Three patrol cars with flashing lights and the crime scene van went speeding down the one-lane dirt road, throwing up a cloud of dust. They drove past our site heading to Otto's house. Based on where the sirens abruptly stopped, it sounded like that was where they came to rest.

I was hoping this was the police response to the results of the bone. I suspected, by the level of response, that the bone was human. Or that they were going to arrest Otto for wasting their time. Another possibility: what if something happened to Otto?

I was torn. I didn't want to be in the middle of another investigation. But I liked Otto and wanted to make sure he was not injured or worse. Even though I didn't find the bone, it was my dog that did. I certainly didn't want to cause any trouble for Otto. I didn't want to do anything that would contradict the story he told the police about how the bone ended up being tested by the FBI. I supposed if he was hurt or dead, there was nothing I could have done. So, I stayed put.

We put the dogs in the basement, snuggled in the tent. And we waited, most of the day.

Around dusk, Otto, sporting his barn coat and carrying

his walking stick, came walking up our driveway. Apparently, in fine health. Still no beer.

Otto said, "As you probably have guessed by now, the bone was human. The FBI called it in to the local police. The police are coming back tomorrow with cadaver dogs and are going to search the area."

"Do they think this is a bone from the same body that was in Anna's car?" I asked.

"No," Otto said. "They checked those remains, and they were not missing any bones. This is another body, probably dead longer than Sally. Stay here. I will keep you posted."

Cadaver dogs found a partially disinterred skeleton at the far back of Otto's property, up against the mountain. At the foot of what was a steep cliff that you needed climbing gear to scale. Someone or something bigger than a dog had been digging there. They found a few bones from the remains that animals must have carried off and abandoned. These bones matched the one at the FBI. More analysis would be done, and a report would be prepared.

Initial analysis put the death of this person at over twenty years ago. I guess since we were not around then, no police came to question us. And again, this body was too new to be an Indian burial ground.

With the subfloor completed, we prepared for the log delivery.

Given all of the gory excitement of recent weeks, I was looking forward to a quiet Halloween. Anna asked, "Do you think I should pick up candy to hand out to trick-or-treaters?"

I said, "Honey, if we get any trick-or-treaters, I'll do the laundry for an entire year." No, I did not say that. If I did, my enterprising spouse would find some kids and pay them to come out here.

"I don't think they get any trick-or-treaters out this far," I said. "I wouldn't say no to a Snicker's Bar if you did pick some up next time you are in town."

On Halloween night, we built a roaring campfire, piling up some of the brush from around the house. The sky was clear. We saw a shooting star arc across our field of view. Anna was delighted. Which meant I was going to be delighted.

Suddenly, we heard this huge bang, like a bomb had gone off. The dogs came running over and hid under our chairs. I walked out to the edge of the knoll to get a bigger view of the valley. I saw nothing. No fire. No cars. No lights, except those of Otto's house far in the distance.

I didn't think there was any mining in this part of the state. But it sounded like dynamite. It could also have been a car wreck, but there were no highways close by. A plane wreck? Otto's helicopter crashing? Mafia? Terrorists? Fireworks?

It had been a long day. It did not appear that we were in imminent danger. Nothing was moving on the peninsula. I added it to the growing list of mysteries that may or may not get solved.

Chapter 5

GRADUATION

*You have to be always drunk. That's all there is to it—
it's the only way. So as not to feel the horrible burden
of time that breaks your back and bends you to the
earth, you have to be continually drunk.*

Charles Baudelaire
"Be Drunk" – Modern Poets of France: a Bilingual Anthology

June 1989
Paw Paw, WV

The boy had turned eighteen earlier in the school year and couldn't wait for graduation. He wasn't a scholar and wasn't planning to go to college. None of his family did. Couldn't see the point. He didn't see the point of finishing high school either, but his Paw insisted. And you didn't argue with Paw when he insisted, if you knew what was good for you.

Other than driving a tractor, the boy had no real skills and no job prospects. He was supposed to take over the farm eventually, but the boy hated farming.

Let his little brother do it. The kid was a loser. Ever since some magician came to the house when they were little, the kid ran around doing lame magic tricks. He could use his magic to grow stupid plants from the ground.

The boy wanted a huge blowout for his graduation. Strippers, kegs, the whole nine yards. It would have gotten him some serious street cred if he could have had a party at Scruze or Dover. But they wouldn't serve underage kids, and some of his friends were not eighteen yet.

There was this abandoned barn out on River Road that was spooky as hell. It was big enough to hold his graduating class of fifty, plus assorted hangers-on.

He and his buddies hauled a couple of generators out to the barn to run some lights and a sound system. They ordered six kegs of beer to get the party started. Everyone would bring their own hard liquor.

Then there was the issue of the strippers. He'd heard that a new club had opened up out toward Berkeley Springs called Kiss 'N Ride. Kind of sounded like they might travel. Or at least do it in your car. He called and offered them $500 to provide some company for a party. He had a deep voice, so on the phone, no one could tell that he was still a teenager. Cash on arrival, they'd said. No problem.

The party was in full swing when three ladies from Kiss 'N Ride arrived. He had been watching the road for over an hour so he could greet them. They were driving a station wagon. Not what he would expect strippers to be driving, but maybe you did it in their car and the extra room came in handy.

The ladies exited the car legs first. Lots of bare, bare legs. They were young; could even still be in high school.

One girl was tall with olive skin and big brown eyes. Her hair was cropped short at her chin. She had a long, long neck, and gazes followed that down to a hefty display of cleavage. She wore a halter top and short shorts with boots that came up over her knees.

The second girl was Asian. Her exotic looks were not something you saw in the backwoods of West Virginia. Petite, she was maybe 4 foot 9 inches tall. She had on a shimmering spaghetti-strap dress covered in rhinestones. No bra. Her tiny breasts barely held up the fabric. Her tiny feet were in high-heeled sandals. It was hard for her to walk in the dirt and gravel, but it made you want to reach out and help her. She was dressed for a penthouse party at New Year's, not a high school graduation in an abandoned barn. *That one is mine*, thought the boy.

The third was a blonde, average height, the all-American girl next door. She was dressed in a very short plaid skirt, a white button-down shirt and a little tie. She had white stockings that came up to her thighs with lace at the top. The skirt was so short it didn't cover the stockings. She was a little older, maybe twenty. And the leader of the group.

She walked over to the boy, swinging her hips, and said, "You have something for me." He handed her the $500 in cash. "That's just for showing up," she said. "Anything extra is, well, extra. Understood?"

"Yeah, cool," the boy said. "Have a beer, enjoy yourselves."

The girls disappeared to work the crowd. Dancing and rubbing up against the boys. There was a collective cheer as the partygoers appreciated the entertainment. The music was cranked up so loud the base thrummed through the ground at your feet.

The boy trailed behind the Asian girl, hoping to catch her attention.

"I'm looking for something extra," said the boy. He had never hired a hooker before. He didn't want to sound inexperienced.

"What you have in mind?" said the girl.

"What are my choices?" said the boy.

"Fifty bucks, I suck. Fifty bucks, you suck. Hundred fifty bucks, we fuck," said the girl.

"It's my high school graduation," said the boy. "Do you have a special discount?"

"No discount. You pay," said the girl.

The boy pulled fifty dollars from his pocket, handed it to the girl, and pointed to his crotch. The girl nodded and grabbed him by the hand. She pulled him toward the station wagon. He was right about the ride.

They drove down the road just far enough to be away from the noise and commotion of the party. She pulled the station wagon over on the grass. They crawled into the back. She had just unzipped his jeans when the side window exploded.

A hand reached in and grabbed the girl by the hair. She

started screaming.

A voice said, "Shut up."

He recognized the voice of his father. The girl stopped screaming. His father stood the girl up beside the car and held her by her upper arms.

The father said to his son, "Drive this car back to the party. If anyone asks, this slut wasn't feeling well. One of the people at the party, you don't know which one, drove her home."

"Yes, Paw," said the boy.

"When you get home, you and me are goin' to have words," said the father. The boy nodded and drove off in the station wagon, back toward the party.

The party was now ruined for him. He grabbed a half-full bottle of vodka that someone had brought and filled up two plastic cups with beer. He headed off in the direction of the railroad bridge.

Within an hour, he had passed out drunk and slept there under the bridge until late morning. He wouldn't have even woken up, except the deer flies were biting him. He brushed one off his arm and stared up at the bottom of the bridge.

He had to go home and face the music. He could be in trouble for a whole long list of things he had done. Thrown a party. Invited minors. Served alcohol to minors. Hired hookers. Trespassed on someone else's property. None of those seemed to have bugged his Paw in the past. Just the hookers were new.

He was a man now. His Paw couldn't tell him what to do. And he knew his Paw was a regular at Scruze. Was this do as I say, not do as I do? But his Paw never told him nothin' 'bout goin' with hookers.

First, he went back to the barn where the party was. The place was a holy mess. There were bottles and cups everywhere.

There was one keg left that wasn't empty. He poured himself a warm beer. Hair of the dog.

He walked the three miles home very slowly. He kicked stones in his path, cursing his father for ruining his big graduation celebration. He walked down the long dirt drive through the woods and stomped up the five steps leading to the cabin. Might as well let everyone know he was back. His Ma sat at the kitchen table, snipping beans.

"Paw home?" he asked.

"No," said his Ma, "but he says you was not to go anywhere 'til he got back."

The boy went to his room, flopped down on his bed face first, and fell asleep imagining the little Asian hooker in the shimmering dress and the things they would have done together if his father had not interrupted.

He woke around nightfall, all sweaty. He smelled like alcohol. He took a shower and put on some shorts. Bare-chested, he went into the kitchen. His father was there waiting for him.

"Ma, go into the bedroom, please. Sit down, son," said his Paw. When his mother closed the bedroom door, his father said, "How could you let that foreign filth touch you?"

Foreign filth. At least now he knew what the talk was going to be about. The boy had heard his father rant about outsiders coming to the area on a few occasions, especially when his father had a few beers or some whiskey in him.

"Paw, I didn't know that there was for'ners comin'," said the boy. "I just ordered strippers from this new club over toward Berkeley Springs, and these three chicks showed up. The little Asian girl took a likin' to me and, ah, I figured, what the heck."

"I don't ever want you consortin' with no foreigners ever

again," said the father. "I'll take care of this new club with the sheriff right quick."

"What happened to the girl?" asked the boy. Something tickled the boy's memory. This wasn't the first time he had asked his Paw that question.

"I took care of her," said his Paw.

"Took care of her how?" asked the boy.

"None of your concern," said Paw.

The boy knew better than to ask more questions on that topic.

"So are you done chewin' my ass out?" asked the boy.

"Go on," said his Paw. "But you better go out there and clean up that mess all y'all made."

Toting trash bags to pick up the mess, the boy and several friends went out to the abandoned barn the next day. While they were there, a station wagon came driving down the road. Looked like the same car the strippers drove.

A giant of a woman got out. Not fat. Just big. She had big hair. Huge breasts. Her shoulders were wider than the boy's. She was at least six feet tall. All the boys stopped picking up trash and stared.

"Which one of y'all called for strippers here?" said the woman.

They all pointed to the boy.

"I did," said the boy.

Maybe she came over to find out how it went.

"I'm looking for Jay," said the woman.

All the boys looked at each other and shook their heads no.

"We don't know no one name of Jay, madam, I mean *ma'am*," said the boy.

"She was here the other night. Tiny thing, wearin' a sparkly dress," said the woman.

"Ahh, there was a girl like that here, but we didn't know her name," said the boy. "She wasn't feeling well. Someone at the party drove her home." Just as his Paw told him to do.

"Who drove her?" asked the woman.

"I don't know," said the boy. All the boys looked at each other and shook their heads no again.

"She a con artist, that one," said the woman. "Any of you boys give her lots of money? She tell you some sob story about wantin' to go back to her own country?"

All the boys shook their heads back and forth.

"She didn't show up for work last night. I think she's done a runner. I'm trying to find out where she went," said the woman.

"Sorry, ah, ma'am," said the boy. "We don't know."

"You are sorry, and you sure don't know nothin'," said the woman. She stuffed herself back into the station wagon and pulled out with tires spinning in the dirt.

A couple weeks later, the boy and his friends decided to take a drive over to the Kiss 'N Ride. Maybe see if Jay had turned up. Maybe the boy would get his fifty dollars back since he didn't get what he paid for. Or maybe he would get what he paid for, his Paw's instructions be damned.

The building where the club had been was dark. There were no lights, no signs. Nothing to indicate that the

Kiss 'N Ride was ever there.

The girl's employer never reported her missing to any authorities. She was underage and in the country illegally. The strippers came and went, so her disappearance was not unusual. She might have gotten a better offer somewhere else or gave up the life. Found the one and settled down and got married.

The boy sometimes thought of her when he needed the right motivation.

Chapter 6

WALLS

Walls: support the weight of the roof; resist side pressure from wind and elements; define the house and provide safety and shelter.

Why did the builder always wear sleeveless shirts? He believed in the right to bare arms.

November 1994

I'd never built a log home before and was excited to see it all coming together. The block and the subfloor were the same as in any house. Same old, same old. But the logs were a whole new adventure.

In preparation, I attended training at the log home manufacturer's headquarters. I also spent a few days at a construction site where a log home was being built by professional builders.

The logs were joined by tongue and groove on the top and bottom, so they fit tightly together. This way, you didn't need any chinking to seal the spaces like they used to use in the 1800s. The male part had one thick square protruding from the log. The female part had two lanes, between which fit the male part. You added some foam insulation strips in between to keep the air out, then bolted them all together with through bolts and caulked any spaces at the end. Easy. Like Lincoln Logs. But big.

The great thing about a log home was that the inside and outside walls were the same. You didn't build a frame, then attach the outside, then build out the inside. Just piled 'em up and Bob's your uncle. Well, and some insulation and caulk and bolts. I was ready.

The day the logs arrived was the fourth big "arrival" for our neighborhood. First was the firetrucks for my water innovation. Second was the drill to dig the well. Third was the police to investigate the bone found by Zeus. Fourth was the massive eighteen-wheeler that brought the logs down our dusty one-lane road that snaked—no, followed—along the South Branch of the Potomac River.

Several neighbors came out to watch the unloading of the truck.

You could order the logs two ways. One was a complete "kit," where every piece was cut and measured to your exact plans. This cost more, and delivery time was much longer. Log Home Building for Dummies.

Being a master carpenter, I didn't need anyone to cut and measure for me. And I didn't need to be searching through a big pile of logs for the right piece. I could just hear Anna reading off the plans: "E22." Like a bingo caller. It seemed like more of a pain in my ass than just picking up a log and cutting it to the size I needed.

With the arrival of the logs, I hardly thought about Sally. Or Cherry. Or beer. Or the other skeleton. I was going to have to find a name for that one now.

My friend Frank arrived the night before from Michigan. We not only lived together back in Kalamazoo, but we had worked construction together for a while. My parents were paying him time and expenses to help with the house project.

I trusted him with my life, but he was NOT a morning person. He was sleeping in his van parked in the driveway. I told him at least four times the night before that he had to be up early to move the van, so it was out of the way when the logs arrived.

"No problem," he said.

At 9 a.m., Frank still had not emerged from his van. I pounded on the side.

Me: "Hey, Frank, logs are due any minute. Are you up, buddy? I've got coffee on the cook stove for you."

Frank: Crickets.

I figured he might be missing his girlfriend, so I gave him

a few minutes to think about her.

Then, I banged on the side of the van again. Frank could be a very sound sleeper.

Me: "Frank, come on. Wake up, dude. It's after nine."

Frank: Nada.

I mentioned I was infamous for playing jokes on the jobsite. Anna was the opposite; she was very serious. She did not like to joke. You joked with Anna at your own peril.

After Sonny and his team left, I was deprived of targets for my humor. But now that Frank was here, it was no holds barred. I saw the perfect opportunity. And it was a way to let him know I was serious about getting up and working before 9 a.m. while we were here without having to have a serious conversation. I hated those.

I knew he kept his keys over the visor on the driver's side. I quietly eased open the driver's side door, slid into the cab, and put the keys in the ignition. I didn't start the van, just turned it one click so I could put the van in neutral.

I eased my foot off the brake. The van, which was pointed downhill, started to roll. I eased off on the brake a little bit more, and the van picked up speed.

Frank burst out of the back of the van, wearing nothing but boxer shorts. He was barefoot and ran hopping on the gravel around the side of the van to get to the driver's seat. He thought he forgot to engage the parking brake. And that the van was rolling downhill unmanned, headed straight for the river.

He yanked open the driver's side door and saw me sitting there, grinning. I applied the brake to stop the van from rolling. Hey, it only moved about twenty feet.

He yelled, "You are such an asshole. If I didn't think Anna

would hurt me, I would kick your ass." He marched to the back of the van, jumped back in, and slammed the door. "I'll be out in a minute," he yelled. *Bet he didn't need any caffeine now.*

On a scale of one to ten, this one was probably a five or six in terms of adrenaline rush for the receiver of my pranks. A ten was when Frank and I were working on a kitchen hood at a restaurant.

He had to lean way into the tunnel of the stainless -steel hood to make an electrical connection. He asked me like a dozen times if I was sure the power was off. Each time I assured him it was.

He inched his way into the hood with just his butt sticking out. When I thought he had picked up one of the wires, I slammed a mallet onto the metal hood. From inside the hood, I was sure it sounded like an electrical explosion.

He shrieked and backed out of that hood so fast. I thought he peed his pants just a little. With one hand, he patted his clothes like he might have caught on fire. With the other, he was holding his heart.

I was just standing there smiling. He threatened to kick my ass that time, too.

In 1994, we still did that kind of stuff on the job and no one would call it harassment or creating a hostile workplace. Like Sonny and his crew, Frank gave as good as he got. It was so much fun.

The plans provided that the first-floor walls of the log home were to be fourteen logs high. With it getting colder, especially in the mornings, we had to heat the caulk over the space heaters so it was soft enough to apply. We had three rows of logs installed when Otto next visited us at the house site.

"Good morning, all!" said Otto. "I see you have multiplied since I was here last."

Anna and I were definitely trying. *Do you think he could hear that all the way over at his house?*

"Hey, Otto, meet my friend, Frank," I said.

"I have information on the second skeleton," said Otto.

Frank said, "I'm sorry, did you say skeleton?"

With all the commotion, I didn't have time to fill Frank in on the body snatchers.

I said, "Frank, I knew if I told you that someone hid a decade-old dead body in Anna's car and that Zeus found a bone from a second body that has been dead for at least two decades on Otto's property, there was no way you would come down and help us."

Frank rolled his eyes at me like he did when he called me an asshole. He couldn't tell if I was pulling his leg or not.

Otto said, "That is true, Frank. The coroner's report on the second skeleton stated that it was a man, probably in his early twenties. The body had been buried for at least twenty years. No cause of death could be determined from the bones. They have no ID. A forensic anthropologist from the state said that based on the shape of the skull, the race could be African American. The police doubt the deaths of these two people are connected, given the length of time each was buried. In fact, they are not even calling their deaths homicides yet."

"Did they find any disturbed ground where Sally may

have been disinterred?" I asked.

"They did not find anything the day the cadaver dogs were out searching my property," said Otto. "Because they have no reason to believe the two deaths are connected, they are not planning to come back out."

"Do you think we should finish our informal search? Finding where Sally was originally buried might help uncover some leads in the cases," I said.

"Cool, I'm in," said Frank.

"I'd like to see where Barrel was buried, too," I said.

"Barrel?" said Otto and Frank together. I had already in my head named the second corpse after one of the other characters from *Nightmare Before Christmas*.

"*Nightmare Before Christmas*," I said to Frank. "I'll explain later."

"It's supposed to rain tomorrow, but the day after looks clear," said Otto. "Can you do it then?"

"Sure," I said. "Will you have Cherry do the catering again?"

Frank said, "Dude, Cherry?"

"I'll explain later," I said.

"We were sitting outside on Halloween night, and we heard this loud bang like a bomb went off. Did you hear it?" I asked Otto. "Scared the crap out of the dogs." And me.

"I was watching a meteor shower through my telescope," Otto said. *Of course he was.* "I read in the paper that a small meteor entered Earth's atmosphere and landed somewhere in the hills about ten miles from here. That could have been what you heard. Curtis and his family have also been known to blow things up on their farm for special occasions."

Not comforting.

"Good, I was worried it might have been your helicopter."

Otto chuckled. "See you in a couple of days."

⚒

It rained like a big dog the next day. Pouring rain most of the day. We huddled in the basement, playing cards while we waited for it to stop so we could keep piling up the log walls. As soon as it did, we were back at it. We would lose the next day to the search.

Anna was watching the river rise. "I think the road is going to flood," she said.

The subdivision was basically on a peninsula surrounded by the Potomac. It was only accessible by one road. At one point, the road was very close to the river. We were aware that periodic flooding of the road could occur. When that happened, you were cut off. The only ways in or out were to scale the cliff face at the back of Otto's and our property, take a boat onto the river with dangerous life-threatening under-currents, or be airlifted by helicopter.

Around 4:30 p.m., Frank, Anna, Zeus, Zoey, and I piled into my van to go check on the road. Sure enough, the water was in the road. Hard to tell how much. No way we were going to cross it. We didn't need anything from the other side.

We stared at the swirling water for a few minutes. Then I backed the van up. No room to turn around. Oh, the fun in West Virginia.

Although we didn't have to go anywhere, if the water wasn't down by tomorrow morning, anyone from outside the neighborhood who was coming for the informal search, like Otto's FBI buddies, couldn't get in. And it was likely that the water would rise even higher before it receded with the runoff from the mountains higher up.

⚒

We all traipsed over to Otto's house and arrived slightly after 9 a.m. the next morning. Frank, of course, had made us late. I figured that we would just postpone until the river went down. It was just Otto and Rob there. But Otto said his colleagues would be there shortly. He sent the helicopter to pick them up.

Surely Frank would now forgive me for not telling him about the dead bodies and Cherry. And the pranks.

Twenty minutes later, we heard the helicopter coming over the mountain. It settled on the pad on Otto's property, and two people hopped out. They crouched and ran for the patio, and when they were clear, they turned and waved to the pilot, who lifted off, heading east in the direction of D.C. That was incredible. Anna patted me on the arm and then patted the underside of her jaw, pantomiming that my jaw had dropped and I needed to shut it.

Because our group was smaller than last time, we decided not to split up but go together in a fan formation. Due to the flooding, Cherry would not be bringing catered sandwiches. Darn. Otto said he had luncheon meat and sandwich fixings in the fridge. Anna offered to stay behind and make lunch. And I bet she watched TV, too. I didn't miss it, but she did.

Otto's wife, who was a retired diplomat, still spent a good deal of time in the city. Advising, Otto said. So, she was not at home.

"Sam, how far did you get on our last search?" Otto asked.

"We did a pretty thorough job of searching the property east of our building site, but the property between the site and your house we were planning to do that afternoon," I replied.

"Good, then we will start there," said Otto. He handed a walkie-talkie to Anna. We just needed one with us since we would all be together.

He did, however, hand each of us a blaze orange vest to put on. It was now hunting season. Although we didn't allow hunting, it did not mean the rednecks would comply.

"Anna, we will check in with you every hour," said Otto.

"10-4," said Anna. "I've always wanted to say that."

"We'll be back here around 1 p.m. for lunch. If you need anything, you can radio with questions," said Otto.

We created a line of people about thirty feet apart and headed toward our building site. I was at the end of the line closest to the mountain cliff at the back of our properties with the dogs. Otto was the closest person in line to me.

I shouted, "How far from here was Barrel buried?"

Otto said, "I liked Sally as a name for the deceased, but I'm not sure I can get used to 'Barrel.'"

I laughed. "Watch the movie," I said.

"We'll pass it here in a minute. It is close to our joint property line," he said.

"I don't want to hold everyone up now. Can we walk over and see it after lunch?" I asked.

"You bet," he said.

As we crossed over his property line, there was a small pond that had formed at the base of the cliff. Not sure if it was always there or was just a result of the recent flooding. I moved closer to Otto to avoid the pond. After we passed the pond and I was preparing to move farther away to maintain our original distance, I saw a patch of earth that looked like it had recently been dug.

"Otto," I said, "I think I see something." I pointed in the

direction of the dirt.

"I see it," he said.

Otto called out in a loud voice, "Everyone hold the line. Don't move forward until I tell you. We want to investigate something."

Otto and I moved closer to the disturbed earth and stopped six feet away. It was about the size of what I thought a hand-dug grave should be, maybe six feet by four feet. In this regard, I was certainly no expert. Otto pulled yellow caution tape from the pocket of his barn coat. The kind you got at the hardware store. This guy was prepared.

"Help me tie this up," Otto said to me. "Maybe fifteen feet on all sides."

We walked backward from our current location until we were about fifteen feet from the spot and made a huge square by tying the tape to trees and brush. When we were done, we headed back to Otto's house.

Otto radioed ahead: "Anna, we are on our way back. Over."

Anna replied: "Everything OK? Are the puppies OK? Ah, over."

Really? She was worried about the puppies? Didn't ask if the love of her life was lying on the ground with a bullet hole from a hunter or the Mafia?

Anna had prepared sandwiches with the fixings from Otto's fridge. Otto called the investigator, Chris Wilson.

"Detective Wilson, this is Otto Rutherford. How are you?"

Short silence.

"I found an area of disturbed earth while I was out walking today with some visitors from out of town. I think you should come out and take a look at it when the river goes down. It has flooded our road but should be passable by tomorrow afternoon."

A longer period of silence.

I couldn't hear the other side of the conversation, but my overactive imagination filled in the gaps: *Don't you folks have anything better to do than walk around your property and find dead bodies from decades ago? I don't have time for this shit. I'm overworked and underpaid. I'll get to it when I get to it. I'm sure it's nothing. Don't call me, I'll call you.*

"Very well," Otto said. "You can come to my house. When you arrive, I'll direct you to the location. I have marked it off with caution tape."

What if the tape alerted the gravediggers that we knew they'd been digging? They probably figured we found the dead body in Anna's car already. No way it could go that long without somebody noticing the smell. They could have family that worked in Chris Wilson's office and knew everything that was going on with the investigation.

As predicted, the river went down to normal levels by the following afternoon. Otto's helicopter visitors spent the night at Otto's house. Otto drove them to the airport in Cumberland to return to D.C. via commercial airline. What a downgrade.

Detective Wilson showed up alone a couple of days later. He and Otto walked over to the jobsite together to get me. Not like they could call. Otto insisted I be present, since technically, the spot was on my parents' property.

"Good afternoon, Detective Wilson," I said.

"Son," he answered.

He had forgotten my name. That was a good thing.

We walked over to the taped-off area.

"Did you do this?" he asked.

"I helped put the tape up, but the tape was Otto's idea," I answered.

"No," he said. "Did you dig here?"

"No, I did not. I found it while Otto and I were out walking with some visitors the other day when he called you."

"Do you know who did this?"

"No."

"Do you know why someone else would come onto your property and dig?"

"No." I wanted to say that I suspected it was the person or persons who put the skeleton in Anna's car, but I figured I'd let the good detective come to his own conclusions.

"Did you see anything suspicious?"

You mean other than the dead body in the trunk of Anna's car and a partially dug-up grave a couple of acres from here? Does this guy have the same list of questions for every crime?

"Did you see anyone lurking around?"

Yep, same questions.

"I'm going to need to call this in," Detective Wilson said.

Excellent, you do that.

Back came the crime scene folks. Sirens off this time, thank goodness. It loses its shock value if it's done too many times. Plus, it was like being in New York City. And it was probably an election year for the sheriff.

We reached the fourteenth row of logs just before Thanksgiving. It was Anna's and my first Thanksgiving as a married couple, but we spent it apart.

I know what you're thinking, that I was going to celebrate Thanksgiving at Scruze. No, I was not. My parents were coming here to see the progress on their house.

Then, right after Thanksgiving, I had some burly help coming to help lift the huge log rafters and beams into place for the roof. Two of my cousins from Michigan, who had played football in high school and a short stint in college, offered to help. Said they didn't want to miss the excitement. If only they knew. My parents offered to pay them to help, but they wouldn't hear of it. Said my parents had helped them out many times, and they were happy to return the favor.

Frank went back with Anna so he could see his girlfriend and spend Thanksgiving with his family. He was going to spend eight hours in the car with my wife. I trusted him. Anna would kick his ass if he tried anything.

The real reason I didn't want to go to Anna's parents' house for Thanksgiving was stuffing. Her mother didn't make it like my mom made it. My parents and I had been invited to the Rutherfords' house for Thanksgiving dinner. I wasn't sure I was going to get Mom's stuffing there, either. But I bet Mom would make some and bring it with her. I could eat it later in the privacy of my own tent.

I was not anticipating that Otto and my parents would be conversing at length before the move-in. However, with the Thanksgiving invite, I was in somewhat of a situation. I had not told my parents about Sally and Barrel or the vandalism of the conduit. I didn't want them to worry. And they were worriers.

�֎

On a nice, sunny, windless afternoon, I went over to Otto's house. Too cold for my sleeveless shirt, which was my first choice for a tennis outfit. So, I put on my second-best flannel shirt. Didn't want to risk ruining my first-best flannel shirt while playing tennis. I asked Otto if he had an extra racket and would like to play tennis.

"Oh, yes, of course. That would be wonderful," said Otto.

"Just a minute, let me tell my wife where we will be." Otto stood in the living room and shouted, "Regina, it's Sam from next door. We are going to get a game of tennis in."

"Okay, dear," Regina called out as she rounded the corner. She was thin and energetic like Otto, with pure white hair and startling blue eyes. "You boys go have fun. I look forward to meeting your parents on Thanksgiving."

"Yes, ma'am," I said. "They are looking forward to the visit."

Otto was an excellent player. On the other hand, it was clear I was a little rusty. Plus, I had the perfect excuse. I was playing with an unfamiliar racket. But my old spin came back, and we soon had quite a volley going.

I said to Otto, "I have a favor to ask."

"Sure," he said. "What is it?"

"I haven't told my parents about the dead bodies because I didn't want them to worry. Would it be possible to ixnay any murder talk while they're here? If we haven't figured out what happened by the time they're ready to move in, I'll tell them then. We can always decide we need to sell the house if it's too dangerous."

"Dangerous? I don't think it will come to that. I understand the situation you are in. Regina and I will have plenty of things to talk with them about. We won't mention the skeletons. In return, I wonder if you are willing to do me a favor."

"Name it."

"I have been wanting to put in a wine cellar in the basement. But I haven't found anyone local that has the skills to do it. Would that be something you could build?"

"Yes, I'd love to do that."

"Great. I'll pay you, of course. Work it in as you have time. I know you have your hands full with your parents' house. There is no rush."

After we finished playing tennis, we walked back to the house and he showed me the area in the basement where he wanted the wine room. He wanted it to have its own climate control system. He showed me a picture of floor-to-ceiling walnut wood shelves.

"If you write up a materials list, I'll order everything," said Otto.

"Great," I said. "We should be dry in a couple of weeks, then some of the pressure will be off. I could probably start it in December and have it done before Christmas." And I would have some extra cash to splurge on Anna's presents.

Chapter 7

TRICOUNTY LABOR CAMP

My long two-pointed ladder's sticking through a tree
Toward heaven still,
And there's a barrel that I didn't fill
Beside it, and there may be two or three
Apples I didn't pick upon some bough.
But I am done with apple-picking now.

Robert Frost
"After Apple-Picking"

July to October 1970
Berkeley County, WV

Apple harvest season was drawing to a close. The migrant workers at the TriCounty Labor Camp would soon be sent back to their homes in the Caribbean.

The camp in Berkeley County, West Virginia, housed between 300 to 600 contract workers who were brought to West Virginia for the express purpose of picking apples because the local workforce was not big enough to harvest all the apples. The workers were not allowed to leave the labor camp or to change jobs mid-season and were required to leave after the harvest so they wouldn't burden the local community.

Many apple growers saw this federal government program, called the British West Indies Program, as the answer to their prayers. Otherwise, their crops would rot before they could be harvested. Although there were a small number of local workers that had been picking apples in West Virginia, these contracted workers from the Caribbean made up about one-third of the apple harvest workforce.

The young man was born and raised in the Cayman Islands. Unlike the lush jungle vegetation of other Caribbean Islands, most of the Cayman Islands were arid and desert-like.

In 1970, the total population of the Cayman Islands was just over 10,000 people, which was only a third of the population of Berkeley County, WV.

Like many native Caymanians, the young man was of mixed European and African descent. He had just turned nineteen and had been working on a citrus farm. Citrus harvest season ran from November to April, and he had been facing several months of unemployment.

He stood about 5 foot 10, wiry and strong. His hair was

close-cropped and curly. His father was a fisherman and was frequently away on the boat. The young man hated boats, but he loved to be outdoors, so picking fruit was a good fit for him.

His cousin told him about a program where he could go to the United States from July to October and pick apples. His cousin had gone the year before. He said that he was provided with basic housing, the food wasn't bad, and the weather was nice. The work was not too hard.

The young man had always wanted to see what life was like off Grand Cayman, where he lived with his parents and six siblings in a small house. He especially wanted to go to the United States. And he would be able to keep his job picking citrus because he would be back by November.

He traveled by boat with several other workers from his country to Miami. There, a bus was waiting to take them to West Virginia. The large bus had "TLC" on the placard, the initials for the TriCounty Labor Camp. They had to wait for over an hour for other boats to arrive and other workers to board the bus.

Some of the workers knew each other, either because they had worked together in other years or because they knew each other from home. They spoke in hushed voices. Most of the riders were silent, staring out the windows. The young man was fascinated by the automobiles and taxis coming and going. For him, the time waiting passed quickly.

The bus traveled for two days from Miami to West Virginia. There was no air conditioning, and it was hot in July. The open windows did little to cool the inside of the bus. They passed through Savannah, Georgia, and Charlotte, North Carolina. Cities and towns that meant nothing to the young man but were interesting nonetheless. After Charlotte, the bus entered the Blue Ridge Mountains of Virginia and finally crossed the border into West Virginia. The young man had purchased a map of the United States at one of the stops the bus had made to track their route.

When they arrived at the camp, the men were assigned to different buildings that were set up like dormitories or military barracks with fifty men, each with their own bunk bed. Showers were outside in stalls. The dining hall sat 200, and meals were served in shifts. Like his cousin said, the meals were not bad. The young man loved being in the lush green of the West Virginia hills, so different from the arid geography of his homeland.

The apple picking was not hard, and by mid-October, the farm that he was assigned to was fully harvested. The bus back to Miami was not scheduled to leave for another week. He knew they were not supposed to leave the camp if they were not working, but he longed to explore some of the cities he could see on his map of the United States that he kept folded up under his pillow.

Another worker told him stories about others that snuck off the camp to sightsee. They traveled by train-hopping, jumping on one of the freight trains that passed a few miles from the camp. He asked his colleague if he knew what would happen if the boss found out he was missing. His colleague thought that he might not be able to participate in the program again.

The boss had not been seen at the camp for the last two days. Since his crew was finished with their work, they didn't need much supervision. The young man felt that he might never have an opportunity like this again. He knew he was expected to marry his girlfriend soon, whom he loved very much. He kept her picture with his map under his pillow and looked at it every night so he wouldn't forget what she looked like. After he was married, he would not be as free to leave the Grand Caymans. So, he decided to go for a few days to see some other cities in the US.

In the middle of the night, when the whole camp was silent and sleeping, he slipped his pillowcase off his pillow, added a couple of shirts, his map, the picture of his girlfriend, and the money he had saved. He quietly eased out of the dormitory and made his way by the light of the moon toward the railroad tracks.

After walking about five miles, he found the tracks and sat down in the gravel to wait for the next train.

The sky was turning pink in the eastern sky when he thought he heard a train coming. It was moving slowly, heading north. He didn't know exactly where the train was going, but he thought he might be able to choose a train better if he started from a central station. He jogged along beside the train, grabbed the handle on an open freight car and jumped into the car. It was empty, and he was alone. He rode the train through the countryside until it dead-ended in Cumberland, Maryland.

He saw Cumberland on his map. He figured it was as

good a place as any to start exploring. First on the list was to find someplace for breakfast. He walked by a diner and peered in the window. He had heard from his co-workers that White people and Black people in America were treated differently. Not much different from the Caymans. But the other workers warned him that White people could beat you up or worse if you went where you were not supposed to go.

He could see through the window that this diner served both Whites and Blacks. One of the doors said Whites Only. He entered through the other door and sat at the counter on the side where other Black people were sitting. He placed his pillowcase on the floor at his feet. The waitress came over and took his order.

A White man and what appeared to be his teenage son were sitting a few stools down but on the White side of the restaurant. There was no line or anything, but it was obvious to the young man where the division was.

The man leaned toward him and said: "What brings you to Cumberland, friend?"

"I was here helping out with the apple harvest. I head back to my country in a few days. Thought I would take a few days to travel," he said.

"Where's home?" asked the man.

"The Cayman Islands," he said.

"Where that at?"

"It's an island in the Caribbean south of Cuba."

"Cuba, huh. You one of them commies?"

"I am not sure I understand."

"Com-mu-nists," said the man, in slow syllables. The teenager beside him snickered.

"I don't think so," he said. He was not sure what a

communist was but thought if he was one, he would know.

"Where you headed next?"

"I'm not sure. I just have a couple of days. Maybe Baltimore."

"You got some kind of transportation?"

"I am taking the train." He wasn't about to explain his train-hopping.

"What time your train leave?" asked the man.

"I thought I would walk around Cumberland for a while and then get a ticket for the train when I'm done."

"You know, my son and I, we gots to make a delivery over to Baltimore today." He pronounced Baltimore "ball-more." "Why don't you ride along with us? We'd be glad of the company and would love to hear more about this island you's from."

At first, the young man had the feeling that this man didn't like him very much, but he seemed to have warmed to him. In the Caymans, neighbors were always willing to help another neighbor. So he accepted the ride with the man and his son. He wasn't sure how he was going to be able to pick a train that headed in the direction he wanted to go. This seemed like a better solution to travel.

He followed them out to a rusty box truck. It had just one bench seat in the cab, so he sat in the middle spot, sandwiched in between the man and his son, his pillowcase on his lap. They wound their way through the town and picked up speed on a two-lane road in the country. He thought they might be heading south, not east, but maybe you had to go south to get to the road that headed east. His map was stowed away in the pillowcase, and it was too tight of a squeeze on the bench to go digging around to find it.

After a few miles, the man pulled the truck over to the

side of the road.

"This darn truck will be the death of me. It's constantly overheating. I gotta go get some water to cool the engine," said the man. The young man didn't know much about trucks or engines. The man got out of the truck, slid open the gate on the back of the truck, and rummaged inside. He came out carrying a tin pail.

"Why don't you walk with us?" said the man. "There's a pond with a little waterfall just through the trees where we can get the water. And it's a beautiful place to see on your tour."

There was a path through the woods just wide enough for one person to pass. First the older White man, then the young Black man, then the White teenage son.

Just a few hundred yards in, they did, in fact, come to a secluded pond that was fed by a small waterfall, maybe twenty feet high. The young man thought it was a lovely spot, as the man had said. The man went to the edge of the pond to fill up the bucket.

"Look, you can see huge catfish swimming under the water," said the man. The young man and the boy approached the edge of the pond. As the White man stood up, he swung the bucket full of water at the young Black man's head. The boy jumped on the Black man's back, and the two of them fell into the water.

The young man was trying to get his feet under him and shake the boy off his back, but he felt four hands holding his head under the water. As much as he struggled, he was no match for the man and his son. In less than three minutes, he drowned in three feet of water.

The man and his son dragged the young Black man's lifeless body back to the box truck. The man removed a large carpet and rolled the body inside. The boy and the man hoisted it into the box truck, rolled down the gate, and headed home.

Several days later, the young man's boss came to the TriCounty Labor Camp to make sure his crew was packing up and getting ready to go home. He called a meeting and read roll call. No one answered when the young man's name was read. The boss asked the assembled men if they knew where he was. They all shook their heads no.

Although the men were not supposed to leave the camp, it happened sometimes. The boss reported the young man to the immigration authorities and marked his name "do not hire" in his employment records. He thought nothing more about it.

The young man's mother and girlfriend were waiting for him at the dock when his boat was scheduled to return. When everyone got off the boat and he was not on it, his mother went up to a group of men and asked if they knew her son. They said they worked with him at the camp but that he was not on the boat.

After a week when he did not return, his mother called the number given to sign up for the program. The man who answered the phone did not have any information but said he would pass along a message, and someone would be in touch. There was no phone at the young man's house, so his mother gave him the post office phone number. The postmaster there would take a message.

Two weeks later, there was no call from the program, but a check arrived in the mail for the young man's final wages.

His mother called the same number again and spoke to the same man. He told her he just signed people up and didn't know anything about people already in the program. He told her he passed along her message to someone else.

After two more weeks, when she still had not received an answer, she asked a neighbor to write a letter to the British West Indies Program and mailed it to an address in Washington, D.C. Every day that passed, the young man's family and his girlfriend expected him to show up with some wild story about his adventures. Months later, his mother received a short letter.

Your son voluntarily left the British West Indies Program in October 1970. He unlawfully left the camp, and his whereabouts are unknown. If he is still in the United States, he is there illegally and will be deported by the US Immigration Department. There is no additional information we can provide.

The consensus among the neighbors was that the young man wasn't ready to settle down and get married. He always talked of traveling the world. He must have loved the US so much that he decided not to return to his home in the Cayman Islands. Perhaps one day, he would. His girlfriend was heartbroken. She waited for a year, then accepted another marriage proposal. His mother didn't believe that he would leave them with no word and waited every day for a letter. But none ever came.

Chapter 8

RAISE THE ROOF

*Roof: the covering on top of the building that protects
the people and things inside from the weather.
It is supported on the walls of the building.
It forms the topmost part of the building envelope.*

*What do construction contractors do at parties?
They raise the roof.*

November to Mid-December 1994

Thanksgiving was uneventful. No one discussed the skeletons. Regina did not make her stuffing like my mother's, either. I ate Mom's stuffing in my tent. Anna and Frank made it safely to Michigan and back. Frank kept his appendages to himself. Anna said she missed me. Anna showed me how much she missed me.

Oscar and Tom, my two ex-football-playing cousins, arrived on schedule to help raise the rafters into place.

The rafters easily weighed over a hundred pounds each. Did we rent a crane? No, we wanted to do it the old-fashioned way. Like the early settlers. Minus the chinking. If I ever did it again, we were getting a crane. Instead, we used pulleys and come alongs to leverage the weight. And good old-fashioned testosterone. I had lots of beer in coolers for after.

Around 5 p.m., as it was getting dark, an old Jeep drove up the driveway. It was Cherry. Anna, as a surprise, ordered dinner to feed all the men. She knew how much I enjoyed the catered lunch at Otto's. I was one lucky man.

Oscar and Tom were a bit older than me. They had been married to their respective wives for several years. Oscar had two kids already. Tom and his wife were "still trying." I introduced them to Cherry.

"Oscar, Tom, meet my neighbor, Cherry," I said. I waited for them to say something. They were speechless.

Cherry laughed. "Hi, y'all. Aren't you sweet to help out ol' Sam here."

Still nothing from Oscar and Tom. I just stood back, enjoying the interplay. Anna rolled her eyes.

Cherry said, "Come on, now, dig in. Bet you're hungry

after all that hard work today. Sam, come on, give me a tour."

I tended to be a bit detail-oriented when it came to the house tour. This was where I bent a spike. This was where my drill bit broke. And this was where I whacked my finger with the hammer. I got mad and threw it off the rafter up there. To my surprise, it went right through the subfloor all the way to the basement. My own dear wife laughed at me. Now I had to fix the hole. Cherry humored me because she knew I tipped well.

I pulled Oscar and Tom aside and told them that before we were done with the rafters, I would take them to Scruze to see Cherry dance. I told them Anna thought it would be fine if I went. "No, she didn't," they said.

We did make a trip out to Scruze on the Sunday before Oscar and Tom were due to head back to Michigan. Scruze was right on the main highway heading into Cumberland. It had a big neon sign flashing "Scruze Club" high up on a pole so you were sure not to drive past. The word "Club" had a pole with a dancing girl instead of the letter "L."

The parking lot was gravel, full of potholes, nearly big enough to swallow my van. About a dozen pickup trucks were already there. Pretty good crowd for a Sunday. There was a double-door entrance, one door outside, the other door inside. This way, the noise didn't leak out. And you could transition from the real world to the den of iniquity.

Frank, Oscar, Tom and I, all big guys, were not inconspicuous as we entered the club. Inside, it was pure strip club. Dark, upholstered completely in red velvet. I never really understood why velvet was the fabric of choice for a stripper club. It was not easy to clean, particularly with sticky substances. Like beer.

Cherry was sitting at the bar. Must be between sets. A

girl I didn't recognize was dancing. The music was too loud. You felt the bass in the pit of your stomach. Cherry turned to the door to see who came in. A huge smile lit up her face.

She said, "Sam, Frank, glad to see you brought your family. Oscar and Tom, welcome to Scruze."

You could tell Oscar and Tom swelled with the VIP treatment. Everybody knows your name.

"Are you having dinner tonight or just drinks?" Cherry asked.

"We're starving. Let's have a table, but not too far from the stage," I said.

Cherry waved the hostess over. She seated us two rows back from the stage. Great visibility for the dancing, and we wouldn't get jostled while we were eating.

A waitress wearing a tiny maid's outfit came over to our table. "What'll it be, guys?" she asked.

Frank and I ordered steaks. Tom ordered a burger. Oscar, who said his wife had put him on a diet, ordered the fried chicken. And a pitcher of beer for the table.

One of my favorite things on the menu at Scruze was a ramp pie. Ramps were a type of wild leek. You could only get them in the spring. They grew in the forest, high up in the Appalachian Mountains. I heard that the firehouse had a fundraiser every year. Everyone went out to pick ramps. There was a contest to see who could pick the most. Then everyone came back to the fire hall where they roasted a pig and cooked up a huge mess of ramps. More West Virginia fun. I couldn't wait!

Cherry did one of my favorite dance numbers later in the evening. It involved very little clothing and leg splits. I swore I could watch it over and over. I supplied a huge pile of singles, and Oscar, Tom, and Frank plied the dancers with dough. I knew Cherry was spying on me for my wife, so I kept my seat and lived vicariously.

A few days after Tom and Oscar left, I went out to pick up supplies and to stop at the post office to get mail. Success, the postmaster was in.

The postmaster said, "Remember I told you about them boys that stole Potter's bull?"

"Oh, yeah," I said.

"I hear they out on bail. Trial is scheduled for the spring. Better lock up your jobsite. I wouldn't trust those two not to raid it."

"Good to know." We kept my expensive tools and any easily portable supplies locked in the basement. Things like pallets of shingles that could only be moved with a forklift we stored outside under tarps.

"How's the house coming?" asked the postmaster.

"Almost finished with the shingles. Just the windows to put in, and then we'll be dry."

"Good thing. Could get our first snow in a couple of weeks."

I needed a break, so I headed on over to Otto's to play tennis one sunny but chilly afternoon. Otto had an excellent backhand with a spin at the end. I missed the ball and jogged to retrieve it.

Otto said, "The report on the investigation of that disturbed earth came back. They think that is likely where

Sally was buried. No useful information about who she is or who dug her up was found in the investigation."

There were no open missing persons cases in the county from the time periods of Sally's and the other body's deaths. If they were residents outside of the county, there were hundreds of open missing persons cases from the 1970s and 1980s nationwide.

"I'm all too familiar with these small police departments from my interactions at the FBI. I think they are just going to shelve this one," said Otto.

December in the mid-Atlantic could be a mixed bag. Cold one day, warmer another. The following day was a little warmer. Anna was standing in the front doorway of the house. I was up on the roof, nailing in the last of the shingles.

Zeus, who was usually always underfoot, was nowhere to be found. I had gone out to the hidey tool pile in the woods yesterday when I got back from playing tennis with Otto and retrieved some of my tools. Zeus was probably replenishing his pile.

Anna called out, "Zeus, Zeus, come here."

We both heard a reply that was most definitely not Zeus.

"I am at your service, my lady."

From the roof, I could see that the smart aleck answering my sweet wife's call was paddling down the river on a canoe. He was at least half a mile away still. But his reply was clearly audible from where we were. He removed his shirt, stood up in the canoe, bare-chested, and waved the shirt over his head.

I was amazed at how the sound traveled in the little valley, especially if you were on the river. Anna couldn't see him from where she was standing. I told Anna to stay in the house until they passed.

Standing on the roof, I gave the guy the finger, which he probably couldn't see that far away. I climbed down the ladder and got my shotgun. I stood guard and tracked his progress until he was well past the house. Zeus appeared from the direction of the tool pile and was sitting by my side at attention.

Maybe Otto could hear us when we were in the tent doing newly married activities. But now that we were in the basement, I didn't think he could hear any longer.

I know I said never to joke with Anna, but that afternoon, I couldn't resist. I had seen some bats sleeping in the rafters over the porch. I pointed them out to Anna. She freaked out.

"No, no, no, no!" she cried. "I hate bats. You have to get rid of them."

"Why?" I teased. "They eat mosquitoes and other insects. They fly around at dusk and are beautiful."

I hated snakes. Anna hated bats.

"Just be careful when you come out on the porch that they don't fly down into your hair."

"That's it," she said. "I am not coming out onto this porch until you get rid of them." She turned on her heel and headed for the door. I followed behind.

I don't know what possessed me, but I picked up a wood chip. I gently tossed it at her. It bounced off her shoulder and fell to the floor. The reaction I got was completely unexpected. She started screaming like death had descended upon her. She ducked her head, frantically brushing her hair with both hands.

"Get it off, get it off!" she yelled. The Z goldens ran into the house, down the stairs to the basement and hid in the tent. They did not like it when Mom yelled.

She slammed the front door in my face and continued to squirm around. I couldn't help it; I had to laugh. She stopped squirming and went deadly still. Then she straightened up and looked at me.

"You did this?" she said in her most accusatory voice.

"It was just a wood chip, honey. Honestly, I didn't expect you to react like that," I said.

"Either you go or the bats go within the hour," she stated. *Oh crap, I was in trouble.*

"Yes, dear, right away, dear," I said. I got a broom and sent the little black bats out into the light to find an Anna-less place to wait for dark.

The following day started out cloudy and windy. The sky was hanging low. It looked like rain. In fact, it almost smelled like snow. We didn't have much contact with the outside world, so we didn't always know what the weather was going to do.

Anna bought a farmer's almanac, just for grins. Some people said that the almanac had an 80% chance of predicting the weather, but I think it was really about fifty-fifty. No better than random chance. Or the professional meteorologists.

On that December day, the almanac said it would be cloudy and cool. So far, so good. We had started putting the windows in, which involved work both inside and outside. I was planning to do one of the big picture windows with Frank, but we shifted to work on some of the smaller ones.

By noon, the temperature had dropped to around freezing,

and a stinging rain started. With the wind, it was hard to tell whether the precipitation was rain or ice. By 1 p.m., we could see ice starting to form on the railing outside.

Being from Michigan, I understood snow. But ice storms in the mid-Atlantic happened more often than snow, especially in the transitional months just before and at the tail end of winter with the temperature fluctuations. In snow, I could put chains on the tires and more or less get where I needed to go. In an ice storm, you couldn't move.

We had lots of firewood, the larder was stocked, and we didn't have anywhere we needed to be. We listened to the tiny ice particles hitting the roof.

After dark, the ice was still coming down. About one-quarter inch of ice had formed on the trees. We went outside, and you could hear branches cracking in the forest. It was like a foggy mist of ice, keeping any sound low to the ground. The trees glistened with ice and reflected the light of our flashlights. We were probably going to lose power.

Anna and I stood holding hands, admiring the beauty of the night. This was the first winter weather the Z goldens had seen. There was nothing more wonderful than watching a dog experience winter for the first time. They rolled in the ice, eating it off the ground. I picked up little chunks and threw them for the dogs to find. Which they didn't. But they tried.

Just then, the power went off. I needed to crank up the generator so we had some lights. But the lights that were at our back inside the basement were gone, and the night was pitch black. Because of the ice, the flashlights threw light into the forest for quite a distance.

Out of the corner of my eye, I saw a light bobbing in the distance. A light that was not from our flashlights. It appeared to be moving. I wondered if perhaps we could see the lights from Otto's house now that all the leaves were gone, and the wind in the trees made them appear to be moving, creating an optical illusion.

"Anna," I said quietly, "turn off your flashlight for a minute." I did the same. I pointed into the woods. "Do you see that light?"

She stared for a minute into the woods. "I do," she said. "What do you think it is?"

"I don't know," I said. "Take the dogs and go inside. Tell Frank to come out. He and I will go for a little walk. Lock the door. Keep the lights off."

Frank was hopping on one foot, putting on his snow boots. I cracked open some hand warmers. I checked the shotgun and put a couple of extra cartridges in my coat pocket. I still saw the moving light, and so did Frank.

In a low voice, Frank said, "Let's go see what it is."

Deer hunters. Aliens. Mafia. Not snakes. Too cold. Bigfoot, maybe. Paranoid much?

The light appeared to be heading for the back section of the property, toward the cliff, in the general direction I thought Sally was buried. If it was the grave digger(s), maybe we shouldn't go. Or we should go for help.

Frank and I consulted. We were the two most physically able-bodied men on the Peninsula. Otto and Rob were probably better with firearms. But to ask either of them to go searching the woods in an ice storm was not the best plan. Particularly if we could possibly have a physical altercation with a grave robber and/or murderer.

We decided to head in the direction of Otto's house. If anything, we could use his phone. Would anybody come in this weather? Good question. We didn't want to risk taking the road and being spotted. But moving through the woods without a light and with the treacherous icy footing was slow going. And we were trying to minimize the noise of our passage.

The direction of the light shifted. Whoever was out there was returning in the direction they came. Which was now headed right toward us. And the river.

"I think we should stop and take cover behind a log," I said.

"I agree," said Frank. "If it's a hunter, he can't see us. He could mistake us for a deer. I love you, buddy, but I did not come to West Virginia to get shot."

We settled in behind a log that was at least three feet thick. It was a huge, old tree. I thought *this would make fantastic stair stringers*. Typical contractor. Your life was in mortal danger, and there you were, thinking of building supplies. I was going to mark this spot and come back here in the daylight to see if it was rotted and if I could find a twin for the other side of the stairs.

The light was slowly moving toward the river. Whoever it was crossed our path at least twenty or thirty yards from where we were hiding behind my new stair stringer. Log.

We could hear a quiet voice. Either the person was talking to themselves or there was more than one person. When they got to the road, we popped up from behind the log and continued to move toward Otto's house.

We reached the tree line at the edge of the pastureland on Otto's property and stopped. We didn't know where the person or persons went. Did they have a vehicle? Did they go to the river? Were they gone or still in the area? We couldn't see the light anymore. If we crossed the pasture, aka driving range, it was possible they could see us.

I knew there was a small hill in the middle of the property. If we stayed behind the hill, it should block the view of anyone on the road or at the river. But then we would be coming up to Otto's house from the back. What if he shot at us? What if he saw the light too and mistook us for the trespasser? With the power out, his security system might not be working.

We skirted the hill, slipping and sliding on the thickening ice covering the ground. Pellets of ice hit our faces. When we set out, Frank thought this might be an interesting adventure, but I could see he was having second thoughts.

We arrived at the edge of the tennis court. I told Frank to stop. I shined my flashlight in the direction of Otto's back door. The door opened, and Otto stepped onto the patio with his rifle. He saw it.

"Identify yourself," he said.

In a voice I hoped was not too loud to carry to the road or the river, I said, "Otto, it's Sam and Frank from next door. Can we come in?"

Otto simply said, "Come." If I was a betting man, I was betting he saw the light from whoever else was out there, too.

Frank's face and mine were bright red from the cold and ice. Crusty ice framed our hats. No lights were on in Otto's house. We removed our wet boots and coats.

Otto said, "Are you crazy? I could have shot you."

"Yes, I'm aware," I said.

Frank said, "You were? And you didn't warn me?"

"I'll take care of you, buddy," I said.

He glared at me.

"Gentlemen," said Otto, "perhaps you can discuss the

risk level at another time. Why are you here in the middle of an ice storm? Is someone injured? Is Anna all right?"

"We saw a light in the woods," I said. "Anna is in the basement with the dogs. I told her to lock the doors and keep the lights off."

"I saw it, too," said Otto.

"Frank and I went to investigate. We lost them as we crossed your property toward your house," I said.

"Let's go to the front of the house and see if we can see anything," said Otto. The three of us moved to the front windows. We saw a light past the road, probably at the river's edge.

"Do you think it's hunters?" Frank asked.

"Let's go out the back door and quietly make our way to the front porch and see if we can hear anything," suggested Otto.

The three of us headed to the back of the house, put on our wet coats and boots, and made our way to the front of Otto's house, slipping and sliding on the ice. "If there is talking, we should be able to hear," whispered Otto.

"I know," I whispered back. "The weirdest thing happened the other day . . ." I was going to tell him about the Zeus and "my lady" incident.

"Tell me later," whispered Otto.

We heard a couple of grunts and several soft thumps.

"I think they are at the ford," said Otto.

The ford was a shallow, flat area in the river midway between Otto's property and my parents' property. I was told the locals called it the "ford" because that was where the farmer used to drive his old Ford tractor across the river to hay the field on the other side. But "ford" was the correct nomenclature for a crossing, regardless of what manufacturer of tractor one drove across it.

We heard a voice say, "Grab the other end and help me with this."

A second voice answered, "Will you shut up! Someone could hear us."

"No one is going to be out in this storm, you ass wipe," said the first voice.

"That's what you said the last time we were out here, and look what happened," said the second voice.

"Just get in the boat and push off, will you?" said the first voice.

We heard the sound of a boat gliding into the river. They were traveling downriver with the current.

I turned to Otto. "We need to call someone. The police. The FBI. These could be the grave robbers."

"I don't know. Maybe they shot a deer," said Otto.

"Or maybe they dug up another body and are moving it by boat, using the storm as cover," I said.

Otto said, "The phone lines are down, as well as the power. I have a short-wave radio. Let me see if I can contact anyone." *High tech and low tech. What a guy.*

"After I radio, let's try to make our way down to the ford and see what we can see. With this ice, the whole area will be covered before anyone can get to us," said Otto.

We waited for Otto in the back Florida room of Otto's house with the comfortable rattan furniture. Otto went to his office. He came back ten minutes later.

"I connected with an old FBI colleague. I also radioed Rob. Rob will try to come now. With this weather, the chopper can't fly. We are on our own until the weather clears. Let me make you boys some coffee," said Otto.

Twenty minutes later, Rob pulled up to the back of Otto's

house on what I can only describe as a monster all-terrain vehicle with chains on the tires. It was camo-colored. Frank was in love. Hell, I was in love. In comparison, my ATV looked like a child's play toy. Men and their toys.

Rob was wearing camo winter hunting coveralls with a hood. A gun was not visible, but the coveralls had lots of large pockets to store a handgun, ammo, and grenades. Typical CIA essentials.

The four of us moved cautiously on foot toward the ford. We were going to feel foolish if this was just deer hunters. We could see evidence of two sets of footprints quickly being filled in by the still-falling ice. Rob brought a camera and was snapping pictures of the boot marks. In between the prints, there was a wide drag mark. Could be a body. Could be a deer. Could be a duffle bag. Or a big log. Or a boat. No blood. Rob took more pictures.

We could still see where they entered the river, but their boat had long floated downstream and around the bend where we couldn't see them any longer.

We returned to the house and told Rob in detail what we saw and heard before he arrived. He agreed that the overheard conversation was vague and could mean anything. Otto poured us each a whiskey to warm us up. I was not much of a whiskey drinker, but this tasted expensive. Would have preferred a beer.

It was too dangerous to go exploring in the ice storm. We would wait until the ice melted in the next day or two.

Rob suited up and headed out into the icy night on his monster ATV, the chains crunching up the icy ground. Frank and I stared longingly after it as he rode away. I sighed. Then, we walked slowly back to Anna at the jobsite, this time on the road.

When we got back, the dogs were thrilled to see us and leaped into the air and chased their tails. Anna punched me and said, "What took you so long? I thought you were dead."

"Ow," I said. "Can we save the rough stuff for later?"

Frank rolled his eyes and said, "Okay, you two. I've had enough excitement for one evening. I am gonna hit the hay."

I threw the ball for the pups to tire them out. Then the four of us retired to our tent in the basement, where Anna made me feel better that I didn't own an ATV like Rob's.

All night, you could still hear branches snapping with the weight of the ice. The precipitation subsided around daybreak. By 10 a.m., it warmed up above freezing.

I figured I better go and retrieve my pile of tools the pups had made. With winter upon us, the tools would fare better in the garage. The pups could resume hoarding in the spring if they didn't grow out of their little game. I needed some of those tools for Otto's wine cellar project, which I planned to start the next day.

The ice was soft, except in shady places where the sun didn't reach. The pups chased after me, and we played hide-and-seek around the trees as we made our way to their hidey pile. They knew where we were going.

When we got to the spot where I thought the pile was, there was nothing. Not a single tool. There was a good-sized pile when last I was there. A couple of hammers, a few screw drivers, some wrenches.

The dogs were zipping back and forth, sniffing the used-to-be pile and all around the area. It seemed they were as surprised as me that their stash was not there. They looked back over their shoulders accusingly at me. I admitted it was what I intended, to take away their prize, but it looked like someone else did.

I headed back to the house. I asked Anna and Frank if they happened to have retrieved the tools the dogs had stolen. Nope. Now what the hell? Did the dogs move it? Did they figure it wasn't safe after I found it? Were they mad that I had been out a couple of times to pick out a tool or two?

I would need to keep an eye out for a new pile when Otto, Rob, Frank, and I went out to scout the area where we saw the light in the woods during the storm.

Rob and Otto arrived, both riding on Rob's ATV around 2 p.m. I fired up my puny, inadequate, almost embarrassing ATV, and Frank and I rode double as we followed Rob and Otto into the woods. We headed toward Sally's burial site. Then over to Barrel's. Nothing was out of place. No disturbed earth. No open or partially open burial sites. No blood. No deer carcass. No piles of tools.

"Are you sure this is where you saw the lights moving?" asked Rob.

"Yes, I'm sure. As they were heading back toward the river, they passed us hiding behind that big log, which I can see from here about thirty feet away," I answered.

"Well, there is nothing here to help identify who those men were or why they were here. Let's split up. We'll head back toward my house. You check the area again back to the building site. Unless we find anything useful, I don't think we should tell the police. It's odd, but not a crime, to be out in an ice storm in a canoe," said Otto.

On the way back, I told Frank about my missing pile of dog-pilfered tools and told him to keep his eyes peeled.

We stopped off at the log where we hid. It was a huge straight pine. I measured and inspected it for any rot. It looked perfect for the stair stringer. I planned to come back with some chains to drag it over to the house. I could peel the bark off by hand with a two-handled curved blade, then put it up to dry for a couple of months before we were ready to build the stairs.

Still needed to find a twin for the other side. With the pressure to make sure the walls went up right, I didn't have the time to get creative. But now that the walls were up and the roof was on, I could focus on more of the creative touches to increase the wow factor of the house. I had been reading log home magazines, and the houses in them were really over the top. Time to let the craftsman in me shine.

We headed out early the next day to get that big log. We were going to roll it. We rode my puny ATV. Frank attached one end of some chain to the log. The other end was attached to the ATV. We had cut about a dozen smaller cedar logs of equal size into four-foot segments.

Frank placed the first of these smaller logs perpendicular in front of one end of the big log. Then he placed about six more logs spaced two feet apart in a row heading toward the house. The ATV was not strong enough to pull the weight of the big log on the bare ground all the way up to the house.

But it would roll the big log over the smaller logs underneath.

As the big log cleared the smaller log at the back, Frank picked it up and moved it around to the front of the line. We repeated this process until we had the big log in the side yard next to the garage. We saved our backs, and the whole moving project was done in less than an hour. Plenty of time to get started on the wine cellar.

That night, we cracked open a couple of beers and toasted our ingenuity. Per usual, we were all tucked in for the night around 9 p.m. Just after 10 p.m., Anna shook me awake.

"Do you hear that?" she asked.

Crap.

I listened.

"I don't hear anything," I said. "What did you hear?"

"It sounded like someone was knocking on the house," said Anna.

"Probably just the wind," I said. "The dogs aren't barking."

In order to stay warm in the basement, we built a platform bed on top of extra blue foam insulation that we used to insulate the roof. This kept the cold from seeping through the concrete of the basement. The little propane heater was a comforting glow in the dark. We settled back down to sleep.

About ten minutes later, I hadn't quite fallen asleep when I too heard knocking. This time, the dogs barked.

"Okay, I heard that," I said. "Will you go see what it is?"

She punched me.

I got up and hopped into my pants and boots. The dogs thought they were going for a walk. "Stay," I said. Three pairs of sad eyes. Grabbed the gun and flashlight. Muscle memory at this point. How many times was this?

I had the outdoor floodlights installed, so I flipped the

switch and lit up the hillside.

I stood just outside the garage door and shouted, "Who's there?"

No answer. I heard leaves rustling and branches snapping. Could be a deer. Or Bigfoot. Same old list. I slowly walked around the house. There were so many footprints from all of the work we had been doing I couldn't distinguish between ours and any recent intruder.

On the opposite end of the house, I yelled again, "Who's there? I'm armed and not afraid to shoot."

No answer. I fired the shotgun into the air for good measure. *Shit, that was loud.* After the echoes from the shotgun subsided, I stood still and listened. Nothing. I also noted that there was no wind. I was thinking that a grave robber was not going to knock on the house. The Mafia wouldn't knock first either; they'd just come in. I had no clue what or who caused the knocking.

I went back into the house. Anna's face was white as a ghost. "I heard a gunshot," she said. "I thought someone shot you."

"No, I just fired a shot into the air for good measure. I didn't see anything," I said.

She punched me.

"Let's just go back to bed," I said.

During the night, it started to rain and continued through until the next morning. I needed some materials for the wine cellar, so I planned to drive into town. I asked Anna if she wanted to come.

"No, I want to watch that video my mom sent." Her

mom had sent some chick-flick that I didn't want to watch.

I had started spending that extra money I was going to make building Otto's wine cellar before I got paid. As early Christmas gifts to each other, we bought a VHS player and a small twenty-four-inch portable TV so we could watch movies in the basement. We also bought a full-sized refrigerator and a microwave. And a shortwave radio to communicate with the outside world, given everything that kept happening.

Still no running water, but soon. I got a month-to-month gym membership in Cumberland so I would have somewhere above sixty degrees to take a shower.

"You want me to take one or both of the dogs?" I asked.

"No," she said. "They can stay with me."

We smooched, and then I was off.

I picked up the materials at the hardware store. I stopped at the gym for a long shower.

I went to the Piggly Wiggly. It was a grocery store, but if you were not from the South, you wouldn't know it. Who came up with a name like that? It sounded more like a kids' play place. The origin of the name was itself shrouded in mystery. One version was that the owner came up with the name when he looked out the window of a train he was riding and saw some pigs trying to get under a fence. He thought of the rhyme "piggly wiggly" and thought it was a good name for a grocery store. I guess I didn't care what they called it if they had beer. I picked some up since we were running low. I got some steaks for dinner that I planned to cook on the grill.

It had been raining steadily all day. There were two ways to get to the house from Cumberland. One way took about forty-five minutes. The other was shorter, about twenty-five minutes. I missed Anna and the pups and was looking forward to the steak dinner. Daylight was fading fast, and it was darker than usual with the rain. We always went the shorter way unless the river was flooding. I didn't even think about all the rain we had had in the last eighteen hours. The van just piloted itself the usual way.

I should note that the usual way involved crossing over the Potomac River on a one-lane, "low water" bridge. It was the only privately owned toll bridge in Maryland. We had a monthly pass. Otherwise, you put your money in a cup on a long pole that the toll booth operator stuck out the window. If you bought a "round trip" ticket, they didn't give you anything. They just wrote it down and saw you when you came back, whether it was one day or two weeks later.

The bridge was family owned and operated. They knew me by name. The "bridge" was deck boards placed between twelve-inch metal rails along the side. No guardrails. There had been instances where trucks ran off the bridge and had to be fished out of the water. Luckily, it was not too deep when the water was at normal levels. The boards rattled alarmingly when a vehicle drove across.

The bridge sat just a few inches above the waters of the Potomac. It didn't take much of a rise in the river for the water to flow over the bridge. After storms, debris like dead trees got caught up on the bridge. The bridge could be closed for days while the debris was removed. When the bridge was closed, an arm with a "closed" sign came down across the road, but it was not long enough to prevent enterprising locals from scooting around and crossing the bridge anyway.

The bridge was damaged by large floods in the past, which caused it to become structurally unsound, per the Army Corps of Engineers. Because the locals kept driving over it, huge piles of dirt were placed in the road on both ends to completely block the road. Those enterprising locals came in the middle of the night with a backhoe and moved all the dirt. Twice. And continued to cross the bridge. Without having to pay a toll because, technically, the bridge was closed.

Butter my butt and call me a biscuit. I was surprised when I got to the bridge that day to see that the water was flowing over the bridge. You could still see little bumps where the water had to go over those 12-inch-high rails. So logically, the water was approximately twelve inches deep. If I turned around, I would have to drive the twenty minutes all the way back to Cumberland, then take the other route, another forty-five minutes. More than an hour until I got back to Anna and the puppies with my steak dinner. In the dark.

I pulled over to the side of the road to survey the situation. While I was considering my options, two trucks drove across the bridge and made it fine. I told you I was a firefighter, right? Despite all my training, I decided to cross.

I entered the bridge, and all was good. I didn't want to flood the engine, so I kept the speed steady and slow. If the engine stalled, I could float off the bridge. When I was about a third of the way across, I realized that the bridge actually dipped lower in the center. That meant the water was deeper there.

I saw water start to seep into the cab of my van. White-knuckled, I gripped the steering wheel. I felt the van go floaty for a second, but I'm not sure if it was just my imagination. It seemed to grip the boards again, and I made it the rest of the way across.

I pulled over on the other side because my hands were shaking so badly. I turned to look back, and I didn't see any other vehicles attempting to cross. There was my mom's voice in my head: "Just because everyone else is jumping off the cliff . . ." Dumbass. Never again.

There were a few other times when I was "surprised" by a water rise. Each time, I drove the hour to go the long way rather than cross the bridge.

I debated whether to tell Anna that her dearly beloved nearly drowned in the river on the way home. I decided to tell her so she wouldn't ever attempt a crossing like that herself. Leading by example.

"Hi honey, I'm home! How was your movie?" I said. Puppies jumping, jumping, jumping.

"Great," she said. "I cried at the end."

I was soooo glad I missed that one.

"Did you get everything you needed from town?" she asked.

"Yes, and I brought home some steaks to put on the grill."

"Yum."

"And I thought we could use some more river water," I said in a lighthearted, off-handed fashion that I hoped wouldn't raise any alarms.

"I'm sorry?" she asked. She could ignore my stupid statements more than half the time. But she zeroed right in on this one.

"Because it has been raining so much, the water in the river was up over the rails at the one-lane bridge. I saw a couple other people cross, so I went for it. I have to say the experience was one I will never forget. With water pouring into the cab of my van. I think at one point I was floating, but I'm not sure. I did make it across. I think you should try it one time." Hoping she would do the opposite.

"You are such an idiot."

Ah, she loved me.

"You can't put yourself at risk like that. Who would finish this house for your parents? Who will make sure I don't have to go back to Michigan?"

That night she gave me a spanking for being a bad boy. Yep, she loved me.

Christmas was just around the corner. Plumbing, electrical, and heating/air conditioning nearly complete. So was Otto's wine cellar, which turned out stunningly.

Anna and I would spend our first Christmas together. My parents were coming to West Virginia for a few days, provided they could get out of Michigan with the snow.

Yvonne was bringing the Christmas feast that we would heat up in the microwave. I set up some sawhorses with plywood for a dining table and threw together a few log benches to sit on.

Frank and I had only the huge picture windows to install. They created this wall of windows in the upstairs guest bedroom. Each window was ten-by-ten feet. After they were in, Frank would head home to be with his family for Christmas. With the heavy stuff behind us, he probably wouldn't be back unless we needed him if we fell behind schedule.

The windows were on the high side of the house. The garage side, where the house was three stories tall. Our ladders were not tall enough to reach, so we set up the scaffolding and then put the ladders, fully extended, on top to reach the rest of the way. Even so, we were going to be at the second-last rung of the ladder to reach the window opening.

Frank and I picked up opposite sides of the window. We

matched the other's pace as we moved slowly up the ladders, the window between us. The window weighed at least a hundred pounds.

Anna was standing in the third-floor bedroom. She poked her head out of the opening as we were making our way up.

"Please be careful," she said.

Duh, I thought. *Last thing I wanted to do was fall to my death with a stupid window.*

"I think I'm going to be sick," she said. "What if you fall?"

Nothing I could do about it until this window went in.

"Sit down and put your head between your knees and breathe deep," I told her. "You can't be sick. I need you to put those temporary nails in and hold this window, or we will fall to our deaths for sure."

"OK," she said. She sat, her back to the wall, and her knees pulled up to her chin.

As we reached the top of the ladder, I asked, "You ready?"

She stood up, brushing dirt from her overalls. "Yes, ready," she said.

The window went in without a hitch.

We didn't fully appreciate how dangerous it was to move the first window up the ladder. By the time we did, there was nothing to do but keep going up. But, for the second one, we knew just what we were in for.

I yelled up to Anna, "Honey, will you get me a beer? I need one to steady my nerves."

"Over my dead body," she yelled back down. All right, looked like I had to do it without a beer.

On the day that Frank was leaving, our farewell was bitter-sweet. Well, more to the point, the post-farewell was bitter-sweet. Frank had been plotting this whole time on how to get me back for the rolling van prank.

"I hate to leave you in the middle of the project, but you are an asshole, and I am not going to miss you," Frank said to me. To Anna, he said, "I don't know how you put up with this guy."

"Safe drive home, Frank," Anna said and gave him a big, long hug, where her boobs, clothed in a bra, turtleneck, overalls, and a puffy winter coat, were touching him for far too long, by my estimation.

Frank turned to me and we did a quick manly hug with three slaps on the back. Frank said, "So you won't miss me too much, I got you some beer. I put it in the fridge so it'll be cold for tonight." A man who knew what I liked.

"Seriously, dude, thank you for all of your help. Give my best to your parents, and I'll talk with you soon," I said to him.

At the end of the day, I went to the fridge and popped the cap off the beer bottle. I walked outside to perch on the front porch. No bats. I tipped my head back and took a long swig. I was lucky I didn't get the chance to swallow it. Beer can sometimes taste a little "skunky," but this was absolutely putrid. I spewed the whole mouthful into the weeds growing around the house. I sniffed cautiously at the beer in the bottle. This beer smelled like piss. I had let down my guard.

Frank nailed me. That scheming guy had been hoarding empties. He filled them up by peeing in them, then replaced the bottle caps. Good one, buddy. I was going to miss him.

Anna came out, and I told her what happened. I asked, "Did you know that Frank was planning this?"

"Nooo," she said in a voice that indicated she was not being completely honest. She colluded with Frank because of my bat prank. Served me right.

Chapter 9

RAINBOW GATHERING

*"This is the Invitation and Information sheet to the
1980 Rainbow Family World Peace Gathering . . .
These Gatherings are Free and Everyone Everywhere is
invited to Come and Share Together. Bring your Friends
and all your Relations to Gather with us in the hopes of
Spreading the True Truth that Humanity is Beautiful, that
We can Live and Work Together in Cooperation and Joy."*

Emma Copley Eisenberg
The Third Rainbow Girl: The Long Life of
a Double Murder in Appalachia

June 1980
Southeast West Virginia

The young woman had just finished her junior year at Bowdoin College, a liberal arts school in the small town of Brunswick on the coast of Maine. She was a Women's Studies major, but she also took plenty of art and music classes. She didn't think her level of art and music creativity was good enough to make a decent living, but she knew she wanted both of them in her life, wherever her career path would take her.

Her parents were both professors at Oberlin College, in Oberlin, Ohio where she was raised. Her mother taught music and her father art history. They would laughingly refer to themselves as stuck in the 1960s, surrounding their daughter with that '60s hippie vibe while she grew up.

In 1972, when she was twelve, she attended the very first Rainbow Gathering with her parents. It was held the first week of July at the national park in Granby, Colorado. Twenty thousand people attended. Musicians and music were everywhere. Art projects were happening throughout the day. Silent meditation classes were held. There were fire jugglers and a fairy camp. It was the perfect bohemian celebration of hippie culture.

The utopian gathering was non-commercial. Selling things for money was frowned upon. Necessities were freely shared. Non-essential things were traded for candy, books, rocks, gems, and handmade crafts. Each year after that, the gatherings were held in different states and grew in size. The young woman and her parents had always wanted to attend another one, but sabbaticals and internships and life in general just got in the way.

In 1980, the gathering was held at the Monongahela

National Park in southeast West Virginia. She didn't have an internship lined up for that summer, so she was going to make her way from Maine to West Virginia. There, she would be a part of the Seed Camp, which were the volunteers that helped set up the gathering. She was looking forward to the behind-the-scenes activities for the gathering and meeting new people. She'd graduate the next year, and there might never be another opportunity. Her parents would come separately from Ohio to join her when the official activities began in July.

She packed her essentials in a backpack, including some etched slate pieces she had made to trade, as well as her etching tools to make more while she helped set up the gathering. She opted not to bring her guitar but carried in her backpack a set of harmonicas her parents had given her as a birthday present one year. There was even room for a couple of books to read on her trip, which she also planned to trade after she finished reading them.

Because she had grown up surrounded by loving, free-spirited people who welcomed strangers, the young woman was not fearful or suspicious, and very trusting. There was a sort of pixie vibe about her. With straight, long brown hair that hung to her waist, her large, brown eyes floated over a turned-up nose. She was not very tall, standing five foot one inch in her Birkenstocks.

When she told her parents she was taking the bus to Cumberland, Maryland, they laughed that she would go from Cumberland to Cumberland. Brunswick was in Cumberland County, Maine. It was a long twenty-hour bus trip. Most of the way was on Interstate 95, through Boston and New York. The bus was delayed by traffic, and although it was scheduled to arrive in Maryland at 4 p.m., it didn't arrive until much later. The gathering had arranged to shuttle volunteers to the national park, but the young woman missed the shuttle for the day.

A typical college student, she didn't have a lot of cash. She didn't want to pay for a hotel. She was so close to her destination. It was only an hour away. With luck, she could arrive there before dark if she could find a ride.

Cumberland was a delightful city in a valley surrounded by mountains. She started walking south on Cumberland Street and crossed over the Potomac River to the edge of town. She had a map, and Route 28 looked like a good secondary road where she could catch a ride south.

She found a spot with a wide shoulder where drivers could easily see her and pull over. She set her pack on the ground and stuck out her thumb. A few minutes later, a man driving a pickup truck with two young boys, about six or seven years old, sitting on the back bench, pulled over. She opened the passenger side door.

"Where you headin'?" asked the driver.

"I'm going to the Monongahela National Park," she said.

"That's a bit out of my way, but I can get you close."

She jumped into the cab. She smiled back at the two little boys who were playing with Matchbox cars, driving them around on the seats and doors.

The driver put on his signal and cautiously pulled out into traffic.

"Are you camping at the park?" asked the driver.

"There's a festival there next month, and I'm helping to set up," she said.

"Where you comin' from?"

"I'm at school up in Maine."

"Are you from there?"

"No. I'm originally from Ohio."

"I've not heard tell of any festivals at the park. What kind of festival we talkin' 'bout?"

She was so excited about the Rainbow Gathering and proceeded to tell the driver all about what she remembered from the prior one. She pulled a couple of the slate etchings from her pack and showed them to the little boys. While she was putting them away, one of the little boys leaned forward over her shoulder.

"Hey, what's that there?" he said, pointing into her backpack.

"Oh, that's my harmonica," she said. She looked at the driver and asked, "Would it be okay if I played a little tune for them?"

"Sure, go right ahead," said the driver. She started playing "Oh! Susanna." The little boys were beaming smiles in the back seat. When she got about halfway through the song, the driver put on his right turn signal and pulled over to the side of the road.

"Engine light just came on," said the driver. "I'm going to pop the hood and see what's up."

She finished playing the song, and the boys begged her to play another. She played "On Top of Old Smokey."

When she got to the end, she rolled down her window and leaned her head out.

"Everything okay?" she asked the driver.

"If you wouldn't mind, I could use your help," said the driver. She hopped down out of the cab and came around to the front of the vehicle, where the driver was bent over, looking into the engine. He stood up and turned to her, holding what looked like a wire. Without warning, he kicked her in the knees, and she fell to the ground. Before she could catch her breath and make a noise, the driver came around behind her and wrapped the wire around her neck. He was a big man of about thirty years old, with a thick black beard. Maybe 250 pounds. She was helpless. She was unconscious in seconds and dead in less than a minute.

When the little boys got bored playing with their cars, one of them leaned out the window and called, "Paw, can we go now?"

The driver said, "You just stay there with your brother. We'll be ready to go in a few minutes."

The boys noticed that their Paw was moving something heavy to the back of the truck, but they were engaged in their car game. They heard a thump when something was placed in the truck bed, but they were not curious enough to turn to see. The one boy thought it might be a tire. Then the boys heard the crinkling sound a tarp makes when their father covered up the woodpile.

Their father opened the truck door, wiping his hands on his Carhartt pants. He got in the cab and started the engine.

One of the boys asked his father, "What happened to the lady?"

"She decided to go on a walk by herself."

"But she left all her stuff."

"It was too heavy for her to carry. She told me she would have a friend come by to pick it up."

The little boy understood that problem. Most things were too heavy for him. Satisfied with the explanation, he went back to playing with his car, and his father drove home.

When they arrived, the boys popped out of the truck and clambered up the five steps to the front door of the cabin.

"Wipe your feet and tell your Ma that I've got somethin' I has to do before dinner," said the driver. He went into a lean-to and started the engine on a four-wheel ATV. He pulled the ATV to the back of the truck, moved the contents from the truck bed to the wagon hitched behind the ATV, and drove the ATV off into the woods.

When they didn't hear from her, the young woman's parents weren't worried. They knew she would be busy getting settled and helping to set up, and phones were not easily accessible in the park.

Her parents arrived at the park on July 1, 1980, and went straight to the volunteer camp to search for their daughter. No one they spoke to knew her and everyone they asked all day had not seen her.

Her parents learned that two other women that were on their way to the gathering had been murdered. The bodies of those girls had been found on June 25 in a state park about twenty miles from the gathering. The girls were hitchhiking from Iowa.

With mounting dread, her parents contacted the National Forest Service. Because there was no evidence that she had ever been in the National Park, the National Forest Service said they did not have jurisdiction. They recommended contacting the state police, who were also assisting local law enforcement in the investigation of the murders of the two girls from Iowa.

The state police also had no jurisdiction because there was no evidence she was in West Virginia. They suggested that her parents contact the police in the last place she was known to be.

Her parents posted flyers throughout the gathering. They handed them out to anyone they passed during the event. At the big silent meditation held on the morning of July 4, they walked through the crowds desperately searching for their daughter.

They reported her missing to the Cumberland County, Maine, Sheriff's office. An investigator was assigned. Bowdoin College was notified. Her parents left the gathering and drove north to Maine. Along the way, they stopped at the bus station in Cumberland, Maryland. No one remembered seeing their daughter. They posted signs there and got the bus route, which they followed in reverse, posting flyers at each bus stop.

When they arrived in Maine, the investigator informed them that no one at the bus terminal remembered their daughter boarding a bus, but there were a lot of students leaving for home at the end of the school year. Too many to remember one specific girl.

By mid-August, there had been no credible leads in her disappearance. The students were returning to school. Her parents returned to Ohio to face the unimaginable reality that they might never know what happened to their daughter.

They followed the murder investigation of the Rainbow Girls, as the press was calling them, in Pocahontas County, West Virginia. Investigators focused on local residents because of the remote location where their bodies were found, but no charges were brought until more than a decade later. In 1993, a local resident was convicted of killing the two girls and was sentenced to life in prison without parole. Investigators questioned him regarding the young girl's disappearance, but he denied any knowledge of her.

Her parents never gave up searching for their daughter. Every year, they spoke to the investigators in Maine. No credible evidence was ever obtained as to how, where, or why she had disappeared.

Chapter 10

INTERIOR WALLS

*Interior walls: define the individual rooms of the house.
They may be load bearing or non-load bearing.*

*Why is a day at a construction site like Christmas?
You end up doing all the work and some fat guy
in a suit takes all the credit.*

End of December 1994 - January 1995

Although the logs provided both the inside and outside of the four exterior walls of the log home, there were still the inside walls to build. We bought wood panels that matched the profile of the logs for the maximum wood look. But I didn't think they had to all be run parallel. So we got creative. Ran some perpendicular on one wall and did a couple smaller walls with the boards running at forty-five degrees. It was wonderful to be warm and dry.

Anna and I decided to surprise Yvonne and Nick with a giant Christmas tree. We couldn't find a tree that was satisfactory on the property. No, we had to drive for an hour to find this Christmas tree farm in the middle of nowhere. It had some sad-looking trees that could have been decades old. We marched halfway up a hill until Anna found "the one."

Puppies: _What about this one? What about this one? What about this one? If I pee on it, can we take this one? Or this one?_

The tree had to be really tall. Anna wanted one that would reach the ceiling of the living room, a soaring twenty feet tall because of the open loft on the second floor. But it couldn't be too wide to fit in the room.

"This one," Anna decreed in a tone that meant she was taking no prisoners. I nodded my head yes so she didn't hurt me. I stood and studied the tree. On an ordinary tree farm, this tree would have been harvested ten years ago. But just our luck (and not so much for them), they had a lot of tree inventory that was now too big for most homes.

"Are you sure? It looks a little scraggly," I said.

"You look a little scraggly, and I love you. Make sure it's

not too tall to fit inside the room."

"It'll work. I don't know how we are going to get it on top of the van and drive home with it. But I can definitely make it fit in the room."

"And look nice."

"Yes, dear."

I whipped out my trusty chainsaw. In ten short minutes, I committed tree murder, damaging my karma so we could have a live tree in the house for decoration for a couple of weeks. I could have gotten an ordinary eight-foot tree with the root ball intact and then planted it when we were done. Maybe I could burn this one after it was dead and dry. At least it would contribute to keeping us warm and increase carbon emissions.

I dragged that puppy all the way back down the hill. It took me ten more minutes to find the tree guy. I found him taking a nap inside a hut heated by a pellet stove.

"How much?" I asked the guy.

"Twenty," he said. I pulled a wrinkled twenty-dollar bill out of my pocket and handed it to him. Couldn't even buy a regular-sized tree at that price. A bargain. He settled back down in his chair to resume his nap.

I had to use a come along tool to get the tree on the roof of the van. Even if he were awake, the tree lot guy would have been no help. He was ninety if he was a day. Anna provided lots of unhelpful instructions. I ratcheted the tree down with tie straps.

"Not too tight," Anna said. "We don't want to break any of the branches."

"If I don't do it tight enough, it's going to fly off the roof on the drive home. That isn't going to be so good for the branches," I said. Or the poor bastard traveling behind us.

Anna brought hot chocolate for us and bones for the puppies that we enjoyed before attempting the drive back to the house. On the road, we passed other people with normal-sized Christmas trees on their vehicles, all tied up with string or burlap. Our tree was flapping wildly in the wind, pieces flying off as we drove down the road, leaving a trail of pine debris. I felt like people were staring at us. More than usual. No one wanted to drive behind us. They passed us even on a double yellow line, which in West Virginia is interpreted as merely a suggestion not to pass.

When we got back, I unstrapped the tree and unceremoniously rolled it off the side of the van. Anna was in the house, warming up. I grabbed the bottom of the trunk and dragged it onto the front porch, then stuffed it in through the door.

I admit, I only eyeballed how tall the tree was. *Measure twice, cut once*, my ass. I had to do a little on-site adjustment. No problem. But no way I was going to take it back outside again to cut it.

Yvonne would be mortified if she knew I ran the chainsaw in her house. It was still a construction site, so technically, it didn't count. Made a hell of a noise. And the smell of gas was overpowering.

I ended up cutting off about four feet into the branches at the bottom. But when I was done, the top branches just brushed the ceiling. I had fashioned a wooden tree stand. Rather than using scaffolding to decorate this, I shimmied it over to the loft and we hung over the side to do the top part.

⚒

Speaking of decorations, we didn't have any. Yvonne had lots of them. Plenty to decorate this giant tree. But we didn't want to ruin the surprise, so we couldn't tell her to bring them.

Anna decided to make them old school. She cut out paper angels. Strung together popcorn and cranberries. She tied ribbons on some of the tools and hung them on the tree. She found pine cones and painted them gold.

There was a little antique/thrift store in Paw Paw where we found these old-fashioned Christmas lights from the 1950s. Five dollars a box. They were big multicolored glass globes and heavily frosted. They showed up perfectly on the tree. I hoped they wouldn't burn the house down.

Some of the dog toys found their way onto the tree . . . and then found their way off of the tree when the dogs realized what we had done. Anna made twig reindeer and stars. I showed her how to use the jigsaw, and she cut out Christmas cookie shapes from leftover plywood and painted them. Not only was she creative, but she was very handy. She used a shiny silvery tarp for a tree skirt. With all the folds and the large scale of the tree, you had to look hard to see what it was.

A couple of days later, I was in the basement and Anna was upstairs adding some more things she found to the tree. I heard, "Oh shit, oh shit, oh shit."

"Anna, is everything okay?" I asked.

"No," she answered, providing absolutely no context as to what manner of crisis I could be facing. I imagined the antique lights had started the tree on fire. This to me seemed to be the most likely emergency, so I grabbed the fire extinguisher and ran up the stairs.

"What is it?" I yelled as I burst through the door, swiveling from side to side, searching for pockets of fire.

"I think it's spider mites," said Anna.

"I don't understand," I said.

"I think the tree had a nest of spider mites in it. The warmth must have woken them up, and now they're crawling everywhere," said Anna.

Sure enough, bugs had found their way to the walls and across the floor, heading for the kitchen.

"Hair spray and some of your spray deodorant. Right now. Hurry. Please," I said.

Anna didn't ask questions, but I heard her talking to herself on the way down the stairs to the basement. "What, is he going to fix their hair and make sure they don't smell bad before they take up permanent residence in the house?" Smart aleck.

She was back in a minute, and I told her to start spraying the bugs with the deodorant. I sprayed the hair spray on the bugs. Spiders have exoskeletons, so the toxic chemicals killed them immediately.

We did this until we ran out of spray. I jumped in the van and drove to the little country store in town, where bug spray was among the one hundred essential things they had on their shelves. We found bugs to spray for at least two days before we eradicated them all.

I hooked up the water lines to the well so at least we would have cold running water in the sinks. No showers or toilets yet. Baby steps. Sonny came to dig the septic field and the hole for the septic tank.

Three days before Christmas, Yvonne and Nick arrived. They had been watching the weather and timed it just right to get out before a storm hit Michigan. They encountered a little snow in Pennsylvania, but not too bad. We had no snow accumulation in West Virginia since the ice storm.

Yvonne was over the moon with the Christmas tree. She touched every "ornament" she could reach. She would keep and treasure the paper angels and the twig ornaments for years to come.

We threw a sheet over the plywood for a tablecloth. Anna filled the center of the table with cedar greens and candles. Yvonne had prepared a feast, complete with my favorite stuffing. The puppies were mesmerized by the presents and wanted to open them all, whether they were for them or not. It was a magical Christmas.

Yvonne brought small gifts for Otto and Regina. We walked over to their house one afternoon after Christmas and sat sipping brandy in front of a huge, roaring fire.

Yvonne ran around measuring windows in the log house for the curtains she wanted to put up when they moved in and all the walls to place various pieces of furniture.

We thought Yvonne and Nick would stay through New Year's Day, but it looked like a storm was heading our way. They left for Michigan the day before New Year's Eve. I was looking forward to getting snowed in with Anna.

Snow was predicted to start falling on New Year's Eve after 8 p.m. Bad for people who were partying out on the town. But for us, our plans involved burrowing into a sleeping bag for a long winter's, ah, nap. Anna suggested we run into town before the snow started so we would be fully stocked for several days. The predictions were this could be a big one, a foot or more of snow. I'd believe it when I saw it.

Before noon on New Year's Eve, Anna, the Z goldens, and I set out for town in the van. Anna had a few places she wanted to go, including a place called Peek A Boo. Like Piggly Wiggly, the name is reminiscent of childhood games, but judging by the items in the window, our time together in the sleeping bag on New Year's Eve was going to be extra special.

The Z goldens and I window-shopped. At least a dozen young girls stopped us to *oooh* and *ahhh* over the Z goldens. What were their names? How much did they weigh? How old were they? Total chick magnets.

At the Piggly Wiggly, we got a bottle of champagne for Anna. Beer for me. Pork and beans, ribs, and plenty of food to last an indefinite siege. When we left the grocery store around 5 p.m., light flurries started to fall. *We timed this just right*, I thought.

As we traveled the winding road to the one-lane bridge, the snow fell harder, and was piling up on the side of the road. Then snow was sticking to the road. We saw no snowplows or salt trucks. And only one or two cars passed by us. We crossed the one-lane bridge, winding through the hills heading toward the house. When we got to the valley before the final rise of the high hill behind the house, it was like we hit a wall of snow. There, the snow was over a foot deep on the ground.

I was a great driver in snow, but it was so deep that it was piling up under the van. The wheels started to slip, and the van would go no further. I got out to see if I could dig the wheels out. No use. We were going to have to hoof it from here.

The line of demarcation for the storm was just a couple

of miles from our house. Everything to the east and south of that line was buried in snow. Where we had been, north and west, very little snow had yet to fall. Stupid meteorologists.

Even if the snow had not stopped us, less than a quarter mile from where we abandoned the van, a huge tree had fallen across the road. In the winter, I always carried my chainsaw in my van for just such an event. But when we got out of the van, I grabbed only the essentials. Beer, champagne, and the bag from Peek A Boo.

The Z goldens were having trouble keeping their heads above the snow. They trudged along behind us, stepping where we stepped. As we reached the top of the rise and looked down, it looked like even more snow had been piling up on our side of the hill.

"Do you think we should go back to Cumberland?" Anna asked me.

"We have to get back to the house to keep the heat going, or the pipes could freeze, flooding the inside of the house. We would have to redo all the plumbing."

"I don't think I can make it all the way to the house through the deep snow. What is it, about two more miles?"

"I have an idea. Stay here." I handed Anna some hand warmers that I always had in my coat pocket.

"Where are you going?" It was getting dark. Snow was coming down hard.

"I have to go back to the van to get some more supplies. I gave her the beer, champagne, and Peek A Boo bag. "If for some reason I'm not back in forty-five minutes, take the dogs and go to one of the neighbor's houses and wait for me there."

It seemed like forever to get back to the van. I put more food into the backpack. I grabbed some rope and two flashlights, then headed back to Anna and the Z goldens. She had wandered back to the fallen tree and was sitting on it, watching intently down the road for my return.

"Oh, thank God," she said and hugged me hard. She looked me up and down, taking a quick inventory of what I was carrying. "What are you planning to do with the rope?"

"If we walk along the ridge and then climb down the cliff face, there'll be less snow to get through. Then you should be able to make it to the house."

"I like adventure as much as the next girl, but I don't have any experience climbing. In the dark. In a snowstorm."

"Don't worry. I'll help you."

"How will the puppies get down?"

"We are going to make a sling with the rope, and you will hand them down to me."

"I don't know. Let's just try to walk the road."

"I'm not sure we can make it, and we could die out here in this storm."

"Or we could die falling off that cliff."

"Trust me, I was a firefighter. We'll be okay."

Anna handed me beer and champagne. She removed something lacy from the Peek A Boo bag and stuffed it in the pocket of her coat. She folded up the bag and stuffed that in there too. I added the beer and champagne to the backpack, which now weighed at least sixty pounds. I was afraid I might be too tired to enjoy the Peek A Boo surprise by the time we got to the house.

The wind was picking up, and visibility was dropping. But on the ridge, that meant less snow, more ice. At times, we slid on our butts so we wouldn't fall. The Z goldens had no trouble with traction. Their paws gripped the rocks along the ridge. I knew I was going to have to carry one or both of them once we got to the bottom of the cliff because the snow was going to be too deep for them.

It seemed like forever to get to the point that we were even with where I judged the house to be. I thought I could see the outside floodlights through the trees, but it was hard to tell in this weather. I tied a rope to a tree and threw it over the edge. Part of the way down, there were trees to hold onto and then an area where it was sheer rock. There, we would have to execute a rope drop.

The Z goldens might be able to make it on their own for the first part, but I was afraid they might go too fast and not be able to stop. Or they could tumble. Anna was shaking her head.

"Absolutely not. I am not going over this cliff under any circumstances," she said.

Calmly, I told her, "It is almost an hour to walk the ridge to get back to the neighbor's house. Whatever you decide to do, I will support you, but if you go back, you go back alone because I have to get to the house."

"I can't believe I let you talk me into this."

I interpreted that to mean she was coming with me over the cliff.

"I'm going to go first. Watch where I go and where I put my hands and feet. Try to copy my path when it is your turn. You'll be able to use the trees as hand- and footholds for part of the way."

"And then what?"

"I'll be waiting for you at that point."

"And then what?"

"I'll give you more instructions."

"I can't believe I let you talk me into this."

I showed her how to create a sling with the rope for Zoey. I made one for Zeus and tied him to my chest. He fidgeted a little, but I told him to be still and he was. I could feel his little heart pounding against mine. Anna was going to do her first climb with a forty-pound golden strapped to her. It would be a miracle if no one got hurt.

"When I get to the ledge, I'll untie the rope and yell for you to pull it up. You do the same with Zoey and then head down," I said.

"I can't do it," she said.

"You have to, and you can."

I showed her how to hold the rope and to let a little bit out at a time. I knew she had enough strength to do this. But fear was going to be a big factor.

The going was easy at the beginning. As I suspected, you could hold onto a tree and place a foot. I moved slowly down the cliff until I saw nothing but rock below. I stopped and untied the rope. I shouted to Anna, and the rope disappeared back up the cliff.

"Okay, honey. Make the sling for Zoey and tie her to your chest. Then follow my path. There are lots of trees to hold onto. You can do it," I told her.

"Here I go," she said, but she didn't sound very confident.

She made her way slowly and steadily down the cliff. At one point, her foot slipped, but she was holding the rope and a tree, so she was secure. Zoey laid calmly and trustingly against her chest.

She landed next to me and said, "That wasn't too bad."

"See," I said, "I knew you could do it. But that, I'm afraid, was the easy part. This next part is going to be a bit tricky."

"How?"

"We won't have the trees or anything to hang onto. You are going to be hanging from the rope over open air."

"Well, it's a good damn thing you didn't tell me that before I went over the edge, because there's no way I would have knowingly agreed to that."

"Yes, dear. But now that you are here, it is much easier to continue to head down than to crawl back up again."

The cliff face had very little snow and not much ice. I was going first over the rocks, so I could determine whether she could make it with Zoey or whether she would send Zoey to me on a rope sling alone. I suspected that Anna would not have enough strength to make the descent with the dog.

I showed her the new rope position and how to slowly let out the line while she pushed off the rocks to come down the cliff. I didn't think the rocks were more than thirty or forty feet, but the distance was deceiving when you were on the bottom looking up. And I couldn't see anything now in the dark.

I tied Zeus back in his sling to my chest and let myself over the edge. I tried to imagine I was Anna coming down. I remembered different areas so I could call out instructions while she was making the descent. I got to the more gently sloping area of the mountain in just a few minutes. I stopped and unstrapped the dog. I put him in a sit command and told him to stay. His eyes were serious. We both were worried about Anna and Zoey.

"Okay, Anna. You know how I showed you to make a rope sling for Zoey?" I said.

"Yes, I remember," she answered in a tiny voice. It involved wrapping the rope around the dog's belly behind the front legs and in front of the back legs.

"You're going to send Zoey down to me by herself. You'll

be able to see her part of the way, but then I'm going to have to give you instructions once she's in my field of view."

"OK," she said, and I heard her voice tremble.

"You can do this, hon. We are almost there."

"She's coming to you," Anna said.

"Nice and slow," I said.

My flashlight beam picked up little Zoey hanging in space. Remarkably, she was looking around like she was on an amusement park ride.

"OK," I said. "I see her. Nice and slow, just like you're doing."

Zoey reached my arms, and I held her tight. I took the sling off and yelled up to Anna.

"She's here with me. Everything is good. Now your turn."

Anna pulled the rope back up and, in a couple of minutes, said, "I'm ready."

I could hear her descend slowly, then stop. I heard her crying.

"I can't go any farther. I'm frozen. My hands and legs won't move."

Shit. "Take a deep breath and focus. You can do this." At least I didn't have to tell her not to look down. It was pitch black, so you couldn't see a thing below you anyway. "I should be able to see you with my flashlight any minute. If you fall, I am right under you and will break your fall."

"No, I am liable to kill you and the puppies. I hate you right now."

"Good, use that hate and get moving. You can kick my ass when we get to the bottom."

I saw her. She was going to make it. The Z goldens' tails thumped on the ground when they saw Mommy, but they remained in their sit/stay position.

I walked my hands up her legs and supported her as she

made the last bit of the descent over the rocky cliff face. I could feel her arms and legs trembling with the strain, but she made it. We made it.

The rest of the way down the cliff should be easier. We probably didn't need the rope, but I tied it to Anna's waist just in case she slipped. I went down the rest of the way holding onto tree branches. The puppies free-formed it.

When we got to the flat part at the bottom, Anna begged me to stop.

"I just need to rest for a minute," she said. I pulled off her gloves and made sure she was not starting to get frostbite. It was not that cold out, just below freezing. We had been working hard and staying warm. I agreed but told her not too long. We didn't want to cool down too much. And it was going to be difficult to trudge through more than two feet of snow to the house some 500 feet away. As I suspected, the Z goldens couldn't move in the snow. I stamped down a little area for them while we rested. They laid down and bit snowballs off the fur on their paws.

We rested for ten minutes. "Let's go," I said. "You carry Zoey. I got Zeus. I'll walk first and try to make a path. You follow me."

We walked only about twenty yards when I felt a sharp burning pain in my butt.

"Ow," I said. "What the fuck?" I turned and saw Anna and Zoey were facedown in the snow.

Anna screamed, "Get down! I think someone is shooting at us with arrows."

I dropped into the snow with Zeus and lay still. I felt something warm running down the back of my leg under my pants. I couldn't imagine hunters were out in this storm. That left the grave robbers who may or may not be the Mafia. We needed to move. What if they had night vision goggles?

I shut my flashlight off. Softly, I whispered, "Anna, turn off your flashlight. Stay down. We need to crawl behind a tree to put some cover between us and whoever is out here." I wished I had my shotgun, but I left it back at the house. Didn't think I would need it for our trip into town.

We crawled about ten feet and stood behind two trees on the opposite side of the direction the arrow had come from.

"I'm scared," said Anna.

Me too. I put my finger to my lips. An arrow hit the opposite side of the tree where Anna was sitting and lodged into the bark. At least now I was sure that it was an arrow that struck me. I initially thought I had been scratched by a rock or tree branch on the way down the cliff.

We stayed like that for what felt like forever, waiting for the next arrow to run us through. What if the shooter circled around and could hit us from this side? They would have to make a really wide arc in order for me not to be able to hear them moving. I heard nothing. Just the hissing sound of falling snow and the wind howling high in the trees.

After half an hour, we had to move or die out there in the cold. I set Zeus down behind me and motioned for him to follow. I gave Anna the "stay" hand signal. I would test to see if the shooter had gone. I crawled on my belly to the next tree closest to the house. Zeus followed. No arrows or bullets. I did the same to the next tree. I waved to Anna to follow, pointing to the tree I had just left. She put Zoey on the ground. Crawled on her belly in the path I made to the next tree. Zoey followed. No arrows. No bullets.

We moved like this for about fifty feet. I estimated about

400 more feet to the house. I stood and crouched over, bent at the waist. My ass was killing me, and I felt a little dizzy. I walked bent over to the next tree. Anna did the same. I gave her the hand signal to stay low. She nodded, tears in her eyes. I could read in her face that she saw the blood that had now soaked through my pants and into the snow. One at a time, we moved from tree to tree until we reached the house.

I went first under the light, unlocked the door, and waved back for Anna to come. She tumbled through the door with Zoey and lay on the floor, breathing heavily. I locked the door and moved one of the benches in front of it. I shrugged off the backpack. I checked the basement door leading to the rest of the house. It was also locked. I checked the basement. No one was there.

I yanked off my boots and peeled off my pants. Blood covered my pants and my right leg. I didn't have a mirror, but I cautiously reached back to my right butt cheek and felt a slash in the fatty part of the skin. Not too deep to be life-threatening, but it was probably going to need stitches.

Anna's eyes were closed. I hoped she had not passed out. I was going to need her.

"Anna, honey, I think I have been shot with an arrow. It grazed my right butt cheek," I said. It wasn't the cliff that nearly killed us, it was some crazy lunatic with a hunting bow.

She sat up slowly and shrugged out of her coat. She took her boots off one at a time like a small child and threw them in the corner. She stood and walked over to me where I was standing at the utility sink, my right hand covered in blood.

"Let me see," she said. It looked like she might be in shock. "Wow, that's a lot of blood but it doesn't look too deep." She started to cry.

"I'm okay, honey. I need you to do something for me. Can you do that?"

She nodded, tears streaming down her face.

"Go get the sewing kit. And some beer. And the lighter. You are going to have to stitch it up. Can you do that, sweetheart?"

She nodded and gathered what we needed. She sterilized the needle with the lighter. She poured beer on my butt and then handed me the rest to drink. She opened the champagne from the backpack and took a long pull from the bottle. Woohoo. Happy New Year. I laid down on the bench in front of the door so she could sew up my butt. I knew this was going to hurt. The puppies had gone to their food bowls to eat their dinner. How could they eat at a time like this?

This wasn't the first time I had to have stitches in my butt. When I was younger, and yes, a volunteer firefighter, I went over to a neighbor's house to help him with his car. My head was under the hood, leaning into the engine. Someone in the house accidentally let his Dalmatian out. I had met the Dalmatian several times, and he was ordinarily very friendly. But he apparently didn't recognize me with my butt sticking out of the car. So he bit me on the butt. He managed to get his teeth right up into my crack. The neighbor's wife saw what happened and immediately called 911. I would have much preferred she didn't do that. The bite wasn't that bad. Now my buddies from the fire department were going to show up and find out I was bitten on the ass by a firehouse dog while coming to the aid of a neighbor. I was never going to hear the end of it, and I did not. Years later, when I went back to visit family in Michigan, I ran into a couple of the guys. "Hey, aren't you the guy who got bitten in the ass crack by a Dalmatian?" Yep, I'm that guy.

I did not expire as a result of the arrow graze, either. Anna sewed me up with about six stitches. Zeus brought me one of his bones to bite so I wouldn't make noise. Hurt like a mother. I drank more beer. Anna drank more champagne. She washed off my leg and applied a bandage to the wound. She helped me into some sweatpants.

I had to warn Otto. I limped over to the short-wave radio. "Otto, do you copy, over," I said. No response. Again, "This is Sam here. Otto, do you copy? It's an emergency. Over."

"Sam, I read you. Over," said Otto.

"There is a bow shooter in the woods. Stay indoors. I was shot in the ass while we were trying to get back to the house. I'm okay. Just a graze. Anna sewed me up. Over."

"Do you need help. Over."

"Negative. We're locked in the house and will ride out the storm. Stay safe. Over."

"Affirmative. Call if you need me. Over."

When the adrenaline started to wear off, I got mad. This lunatic could have killed one of the dogs. Or Anna. Or broken the beer bottles. Not only was I too tired to enjoy the Peek A Boo surprise, but my ass was out of commission.

Anna said, "We have to leave here. It is too dangerous. We can't stay."

"I will not be run out of town by some idiots," I replied. "I respect your wishes, and I'll take you home to your parents as soon as we can retrieve the van and drive out of here. You can stay there until I finish the house and solve this problem. Problems."

Anna cried herself to sleep that night and I spooned her, lying on my left side because of my injured right butt cheek. The Z goldens were not sure what was wrong but knew it was serious.

By the time it was all done, the storm dropped almost three feet of snow. More than the total average annual snowfall in the county in less than two days. The power went out sometime during the night. When the sun popped out, we heard an engine getting closer to the house. Anna spent the morning staring out into the snow, still recovering from shock. Or maybe standing guard. Z goldens at her feet, Zoey's head resting on her foot.

Rob and Otto came zooming up the drive on a snowmobile, pulling an empty sled. The Z goldens started barking. Rob and Otto stopped at the top of the rise and shouted, "Sam, Anna, it's Otto and Rob. Don't shoot."

Anna opened the front door and waved for them to come in.

"We were worried about you," said Otto. He gave Anna a hug, which she accepted stiffly. He gave me a meaningful look. "We want to hear all about what happened to you out there, but I want to get some organizational things sorted first. It's not safe for you to be here on your own. Regina and I want you to come to our house and stay, at least until we have a better understanding of what is happening and the snow is gone. I'm going to help you winterize the house and pack up your things. You can ride over on the snowmobile. Rob and I will walk over. I'm not going to take no for an answer."

I believed him.

"You can't walk through this much snow," I said. The expert from Michigan.

"We have snowshoes," said Rob. "It won't be a problem."

Of course they did.

"I can see you are limping. Just tell me what to do and what to pack, and we'll get everything ready," said Otto.

I looked at Anna to see what she thought about their proposal. I saw relief and tears welling in her eyes.

I instructed them on draining the water and filling the traps up with antifreeze. We threw some clothes into a duffle bag. We emptied what food was in the fridge. We grabbed a forty-pound bag of dog food. Everything, dogs included, got loaded onto the sled. I, however, was not going to be able to sit on the snowmobile with my punctured butt.

"Who owns the snowmobile?" I asked.

"I do," Rob said.

"I don't suppose you have a jet ski, too," I said to Rob.

"I do. Can't wait to take it out on the river when the weather gets warm again," said Rob. What a guy.

"Anna, are you good to drive the snowmobile?" I asked.

Her eyes were saying *why can't you drive the snowmobile*, and then, wait for it; there it was. She realized I could not sit.

"Sure, no problem. Used to drive them up at my cousin's place in the U P all the time," she said. I would stand on the rails behind her. Still was gonna hurt.

"While someone was shooting arrows at us, one of them missed and lodged in a tree," I said. "We need to go and retrieve it. Maybe it will help us identify this maniac."

"The snowmobile won't make it through the woods. We'll have to go with the snowshoes," said Rob. "Otto and I will go."

"But you don't know where we were," I said.

"You are in no condition today to walk out into the snow with your wound. I think I can find the spot," said Anna. "You were bleeding, and I saw blood in the snow. Maybe we can still see it."

I highly doubted it with all the snow we got. But I could see Anna was moving past the shock, and I didn't want to jeopardize the progress. Even I was not sure where we were, exactly. It was pitch black. But maybe heading back out to the scene could give her PTSD. Being in the woods at all could give her PTSD. We would find out.

We stood on the porch, facing the back of the property. I gave a general description of where I thought we were. Almost straight back from the house. To the west of the electricity hook-up. Maybe thirty yards from the base of the mountain.

"I only have two pairs of snowshoes. Anna and I will go out and see if we can find anything," said Rob. "Otto, stay with Sam. Sam, don't tell him the story until we are at Otto's house, or you are going to have to repeat the whole thing for me."

Everybody thought they could just come in here and boss around the invalid. Geesh.

"Anna, have you used snowshoes before?" Rob asked.

"Yup," she said. "U, P."

"Copy that," answered Rob.

Off they went into the blinding white woods glistening in the sun. While we waited, Otto admired the birch cabinets I was making by hand. I told him the plans for the staircase to the upper floor and the huge log I found the night of the ice storm. I had ordered four-inch-thick blocks of birchwood for the steps, which I would hand-notch into the logs. I also told him about the plans for the railings. Hand-hewn branches. I would do the same outdoors with some steps leading from the garage to the backyard. He knew just how to distract me.

Rob and Anna returned about half an hour later. I actually thought I heard her laugh on the porch at something Rob said.

"I'm sorry," said Rob. "We didn't find anything. There

was no arrow left in any of the trees. We knew you were waiting, so we didn't do a close inspection of each tree for an arrow mark. We will have to do that when the snow melts and you are moving a little better."

Maniac must have retrieved the arrow. Or it fell off and got buried in the snow. We were still no closer to finding who or why someone was doing this.

The sled was loaded with our essentials. The dogs hopped on without an invitation. They didn't want to be left behind and loved to ride. They perched on top of the stuff, finding strong footholds and smiling from ear to ear. Anna slid onto the driver's seat of the snowmobile and I got on behind her, standing to minimize the trauma to my butt. Otto and Rob had on their snowshoes, and Otto had some poles that looked like they were for skiing.

"You got this?" I asked Anna.

"Don't worry about a thing," she said. "I'll go slow to try to minimize the bumps."

"I'm not sure about that strategy. Slow or fast, I am still going to feel every bump. Maybe fast will get it over quicker," I answered.

"OK," she said. "You just let me know once we get going."

We drove down the driveway and onto the road. The river was not frozen over. It looked like it was running high.

"How's the speed?" Anna asked.

I wanted to moan with each bump, but I put on a brave face. "This is good," I answered.

We arrived at Otto's house. Regina was waiting for us on the porch. Anna did a great job of piloting the snowmobile, and she pulled right up next to the front porch. The dogs hopped off and ran to fawn all over Regina. She had a treat in her pocket for each of them. Anna got off the snowmobile next and gave me a hand to help me down. I gingerly stepped off the machine with my left foot first to protect the right butt injury. We moved slowly into the house. The puppies ran off to the kitchen, where they found a big bowl of water Regina had put on the floor for them.

Regina said, "Anna, Sam, I want you to make yourselves at home. I've set up one of the guest bedrooms for you at the front of the house upstairs. I know you don't want to go up there right now. There's hot cider in the warmer in the kitchen and some snacks. Sam, get comfortable however you need to. I'm sure Otto and Rob will be along any minute."

I reclined on the sofa in front of a roaring fire. The dogs found me, whimpered twice, then ran barking to the front door. Otto and Rob had arrived and were stomping the snow off their boots.

"Sam, let me get the sled unpacked and then let's debrief," said Otto. Holy crap, he wants me to take off my underwear? No way I was showing this war wound to anyone but Anna.

Anna, who was sitting on the sofa by my head, stood and said, "I'll help you unload."

Anna, Rob, and Otto went back outside and made a chain. They passed each item from one to the other to minimize the travel distance in the snow. Regina busied herself stashing things and giving directions. With the sled unpacked and everything stowed in its place, everyone settled around the fire. Otto handed me a beer. For medicinal purposes, he said. The silver lining of getting shot in the ass? I could drink as much beer as I wanted.

I told the story of what happened the day before.

"Did you see anyone?" Rob asked.

"No one," I answered. "It was pitch black, and with the snow, you couldn't see anything other than vague shapes more than four feet away."

Otto said, "This whole situation has gotten much more dangerous. Before, there did not appear to be any imminent threat of bodily harm. But with a direct attack, we have an urgent need to identify the perpetrator or perpetrators."

"But how?" I asked. "There's very little information to go on."

"I want to propose something for discussion," said Rob. "It is not without some risk. But if it works, it could really help us. I think we should loop in Cherry. The risk is that she might have loyalty to the perps that we are unaware of. But she has a good heart, and I think if she is not aligned with the bad guys, that she would be willing to help us. She knows almost everybody in town and maybe she can find someone who knows something. If it is a local person doing this, someone is bound to know."

"Maybe we can even offer a reward," said Otto. "I know this community needs money. I don't know how some of these folks make ends meet. Cherry can make it quietly known to the people she talks to."

"I've got twenty bucks," I said, digging around in my left pocket, far away from my injured butt cheek.

"A reward is a great idea," said Rob. "The more substantial it is, the faster we might shake loose the information we need."

"I think I have a ten," said Anna.

"Bless your heart," said Regina. "You hold onto your money, dear. We can cover the reward."

"We don't want it to be too big, either," said Otto. "That could bring with it other problems we don't need to be dealing with."

"Do you think $1,000 is reasonable?" said Rob.

"Yes, good," said Otto.

"What if Cherry, God forbid, is close to the person doing this?" I asked.

"Then the fact that we are applying pressure will make them nervous. Maybe they will make a mistake. Or maybe they will show themselves if they come after us," said Otto.

Rob asked, "So are we all agreed to bring Cherry in on this?" He had me at Cherry, but I think I was biased again.

All heads nodded.

"Should we ride over to her place tomorrow under the excuse of checking on her?" asked Otto.

No, not tomorrow. There was no way I could ride a snowmobile tomorrow. I needed more time to heal. And I wanted to be there for this discussion.

"Do you think we can wait until my butt isn't so sore? I don't think she'll be able to talk to anyone until the snow disappears. Can't even get down the road," I said.

"Well, we should go over to check on her, and it will be quiet with no interruptions if we do it tomorrow. And it would give her time to consider the request," said Otto.

Or alert the maniac(s) with smoke signals.

"It's okay, honey," Anna said, patting my arm. "I know you want to be there, but I'll go and be your eyes and ears. I'll be able to tell if she's hiding something. Women's intuition."

Not really the point, but if I doth protest too much, Anna could get suspicious of my true intentions and withdraw her consent to my occasional Scruze visits.

Regina made a delicious stew for dinner with thick gravy that we mopped up with crusty bread. I ate mine reclining. We played a mini backgammon tournament after dinner. I fell asleep on the sofa. Anna covered me with a quilt, and she and the dogs went up to the guest bedroom. Otto and Rob talked in hushed tones in the foyer.

"I think we need to keep watch tonight," said Rob. "Whether the person is local or not, I don't think they could have gotten far in this storm and could come back."

"With the power out and the security system not functioning, that's going to mean staying up," said Otto.

"We can go to sleep when it gets light," said Rob. "I'll sleep for a few hours, then set up some old-school alerts around the property tomorrow before we head over to Cherry's. Have you heard anything on when they will be out to clear the roads?"

"I forgot this is your first winter here," said Otto. "The county doesn't have any snowplows. This storm walloped everything from here to D.C. I don't think the road will be clear until the snow melts."

"Great," said Rob. "Any idea what the weather forecast is?"

"I was on the shortwave before we left for Sam's house this morning, and they were saying temps could remain below freezing for the next four days. Then a warming trend is predicted," said Otto.

"We'll let Sam and Anna get a good night's rest tonight. Then we can set up four-hour shifts tomorrow night," said Rob.

The night passed without incident.

I awoke to the smell of fresh bacon and coffee. Anna had placed a steaming cup on the coffee table by the sofa along with three aspirins. What an angel. I could see by the light in the room that the sun had risen higher in the sky. An antique grandfather clock on the other side of the room chimed 10 a.m. I moved my right leg a few inches. Agony.

Couch potato again for me today. I could hear Regina in the kitchen scrambling eggs and frying up the bacon. The fire was going strong in the fireplace. I slept like a rock. Getting shot will do that to a guy.

Anna brought me a plate of eggs and bacon with toast and a glass of orange juice.

"Good morning," Anna said. "How'd you sleep?"

"As well as any guy who has been shot in the ass with an arrow," I answered.

"Technically, it only grazed your ass," replied Anna with a twinkle in her eye.

"Very well, a guy with an arrow-grazed ass," I amended. "Where are the Z puppies?"

"I've been trying to distract them to let you sleep in a little," said Anna. "Regina has made them their very own breakfast that does not involve their dry dog food. They don't even know who we are anymore."

"Are Otto and Rob up?"

"I haven't seen them yet. I understood from Regina that they stood watch all night and went to grab a few hours of sleep as soon as it got light."

"Why didn't someone wake me?"

"You needed to sleep. You can offer to help tonight. It doesn't look to me like the snow has melted any since yesterday."

I saved a couple pieces of my bacon for Zoey and Zeus. They came in to lay by me next to the sofa for a post-breakfast snooze. I knew they would have room for just one more tiny morsel of bacon. And they did.

I could hear first Otto and then Rob making their way into the kitchen. They followed each other into the living room with cups of coffee and sat down.

I said, "I heard you stood watch all night. I wish you would have woken me."

Otto replied, "Don't worry. You won't miss out on all the fun. We can take shifts tonight. Rob is going to go out and set some booby traps around the perimeter of the house to give us some warning while the security system is out. Then we are going to head over to Cherry's house."

"What kind of booby traps?" I asked.

Anytime anyone said "booby," my mind automatically thought "boobs." Pleasant thoughts. But booby traps were not pleasant. That wonderful expression came from the traps that hungry sailors set for little seabirds known as boobies. So, no boobs. Deep pits covered with bamboo. Grenades. Buckets of acid falling from the trees. Metal bear traps that ripped off your legs with metal teeth when you stepped on them.

"We don't have a lot of resources," said Rob. "I'll improvise with some tin cans on a wire, that kind of thing. Just something to give us a heads up if someone tries to approach the house."

"Do I need to keep the dogs from wandering too far?" I asked. I worried that he was planning the acid but just not telling me.

"No, it shouldn't be anything that will hurt them," he said. *Whew. Right?*

I had to use the little boy's room. I stood up and limped to the bathroom. Slow going.

Anna asked, "Do you need me to look at your wound?"

"My god, woman, you have an open invitation to look at my butt anytime," I said. She blushed prettily.

"Sam, you are a pig," she said. *And you love it*, I thought. "I'll change the bandage when we get back from Cherry's house."

When Rob came back from putting out booby traps, Rob and Otto fired up the snowmobile. Anna hopped on behind Otto, and off they went to Cherry's house, leaving me behind with the Z goldens. Regina was in the library reading a book. I paged aimlessly through a Field and Stream magazine. I gave the goldens belly rubs. I got up slowly to use the restroom again. The Z goldens followed me. I paced around the living room, trying to stretch my good leg. I got two more aspirins while I was up. Two hours passed until I heard the snowmobile pull up and boots stomp on the front porch.

"Tell me everything," I said, greeting the returning team.

"I need water," said Anna.

"I need coffee," said Rob.

"I need whiskey," said Otto.

Everyone gathered their beverage of choice and sat down in the living room. Regina came in from the library with a glass of white wine. Somebody handed me a beer.

"How is Cherry doing?" Regina asked.

"Everything is fine at her house. She has plenty of food and wood. The generator is working," said Otto.

"She has a dance studio in her house, and she was practicing a new dance routine," Anna said.

Why, oh why, did the universe have to bite me in the ass? I sat quietly with no response in case Anna was testing me. My eyebrows were raised in a manner that I hoped would encourage them to continue the story.

"We told her what happened during the ice storm and this snowstorm," Otto said.

"She said it was hard for her to believe that anyone local

would bury bodies. Or deliberately shoot at a human, even if they were not crazy about the new development. Her opinion was that it was either someone from out of town or a hunting accident," explained Anna.

"We told her that we wanted to take a more active role in finding out why these events occurred and asked if she would help us by putting the word out about the $1,000 reward for information," said Rob.

"She said she would be happy to do it if we paid her $200," said Anna. "I was a little taken aback. So mercenary."

"I think she's quite the businesswoman. Looking out for herself," I said. "At least she didn't say no. Did she hesitate at all or seem like she knew something she wasn't telling you?"

"Not at all. She seemed excited to be an active part in solving the mystery or mysteries," said Anna. "But I bet she's an exceptional actress."

Hmm-hmm. Don't stop, don't stop, don't stop. Yep, I visualized that whole scene in my mind. Eyebrows plastered in the upright position. Please continue.

"I don't think we have much of a choice at this point," said Otto. "The hook is set and can deliver the catch in two ways. One, someone provides us with information. Or two, someone comes after us. We have to be on alert until we know which way this is going to go."

Four days passed in monotony. My arrow wound was healing. I stood guard four hours each night, taking shifts with the others. Anna and Regina cooked marvelous meals in the kitchen. I worried whether the food would run out, but Otto told us he had plenty of meat in the freezer and the pantry was stocked with pasta, potatoes, and winter vegetables. Rob went out on the snowmobile every day to check on his house and the construction site.

The Z goldens ran on top of the crusty snow, only occasionally sinking in up to their eyeballs. They played a game to see who could stay on top of the snow the longest.

On the fourth day, the weather broke, and it stayed above freezing both during the day and at night. The snow started to melt. The river started to rise.

Rob returned from one of his security runs driving a Humvee, which I had only read about and never seen in person. It had a plow on the front and chains on the wheels. He managed to plow a narrow path from his house to Otto's house. He came in for a snack, then went back out to try to get the rest of the road done, at least to the point where it ran closest to the river.

Phone service was restored. Otto called one of the neighbors nearest to where we had abandoned my van and asked them to check on it.

In a couple more days, the snow had melted enough that trucks with chains could make it all the way to the main road into Cumberland. One of Cherry's regulars came to pick her up in his truck to take her to work. Word of the reward would now be spread more widely among the community.

My butt was much improved. Anna and I returned to work on the house during the day but came back to Otto's house at night for safety. The snow was slowly melting away but tended to refreeze at night, creating dangerous black ice. One good thing was that it made it difficult for anyone to come out to our neighborhood during the night.

Anna and I and the Z goldens walked in the tire ruts in the road carrying shovels to dig out my van. Rob came with his Hummer and plowed out our driveway so I could park the van next to the house. Anna spread sand on the steep part of the driveway, and I made it to the top on the first try. Rob was standing by in case I needed a tow.

One evening when we were all sitting around at Otto's house after dinner, Otto told us about a conversation he had with Detective Smith. Detective Smith said that a "source" told him that a concerned citizen was offering a reward for information regarding the bodies found in our neighborhood, and he wondered whether we knew anything about it.

"I told him I thought it was an interesting idea, and I hoped it would help them in their investigation," said Otto. "He told me that if any other concerned citizens were thinking of doing likewise, they would be well advised to discuss it with him first or face prosecution for interfering with his investigation."

An investigation that had no new leads and basically no information. Ooh, we were scared.

"It's a good indicator that the information is circulating through the community," said Rob.

"I told him about Sam getting shot in the rear with an arrow during the snowstorm, and he said you should go down to the station and file a complaint," said Otto.

"I would rather have him focused on those dead bodies," I said. "Anna and I didn't see anything, and I didn't even have to go to the hospital, so it is not like it is going to be a high priority for him."

Chapter 11

FINISH WORK

Finish work: the final stage of construction.
It includes cabinetry, woodwork, flooring,
fixtures, and appliances.

There's this great construction joke,
but I'm still working on it.
Gotta hammer out a few kinks
and nail the delivery
so I don't screw it up.

February 1995

I loved each stage of putting up a building, but I think the finish work was my favorite. The cabinetry set the tone for the kitchen, which was enhanced by the countertops. The light fixtures made the house look ready to be lived in. Warm and inviting. It was progress toward the end in smaller steps and sometimes seemed to take the longest.

When all that was left of the three feet of snow were a few dirty piles along the road and some patches in permanent shade, we convened the usual suspects for a search party. We wanted to try to find that arrow that had missed us and lodged in the tree. We started at the back of my parents' lot with our backs to the mountain. We formed a line of searchers ten feet apart and slowly moved toward the back of my parents' house, checking each tree for evidence of damage and the ground for a fallen arrow.

About halfway between the mountain and the house, I saw a tree with what appeared to be fresh bark damage. The damage was on the mountain-facing side of the tree, where the arrow would have lodged, about a man's chest height from the ground. There was an unmelted pile of snow at the base of the tree.

Rob reached into his backpack and pulled out a folding shovel. What a guy. He dug through the few inches of snow that was left and uncovered a stick. Not a stick. An arrow. Next out of his endless Mary Poppins-like backpack was a large garbage bag. He picked up the arrow, placing it gently inside the bag and wrapping it closed. He sealed the bag closed with duct tape. I wondered if he had any beef jerky in there. I was getting hungry.

We continued the search just in case this was an arrow from another hunter out hunting in our woods. Nothing else was found. We all returned to Otto's house for an adult beverage of choice.

Rob asked, "Should we send this to the FBI to analyze or turn it in to Detective Smith?"

"Or go around to local archery suppliers and ask ourselves?" I said.

If the arrow was sourced locally, a store owner might know who bought it. If it was handmade, maybe they knew who made it. These types of resources would be more likely to be accessible by Detective Smith, should he be inclined to expend the effort. But this arrow was not necessarily connected to a crime unless I bothered to file a complaint.

The FBI would investigate if Otto asked them. They could check for prints but might not have access to the local information. We decided that we would first have the FBI run the prints. If there were no prints or if the prints were not identifiable to a person, then one of us would visit some local archery shops.

We were assembled at Otto's house for dinner one evening when the report on the arrow fingerprints came in. There were two partial prints, but they did not match any in the database.

Rob, the archery expert, was appointed to visit local hunting shops with the arrow. Regina pulled out the Yellow Pages. In 1994, we used a thick yellow book to find the businesses we needed. Or, in a pinch, it could be used as a booster seat for a toddler at the dinner table. The book listed all business phone numbers by category, and some businesses placed larger ads to advertise their services. There were four shops listed within thirty miles of our location. Two of the archery shops had quarter-page ads. The other two just had their name, address, and phone number.

Rob started at the shop with a print ad in Cumberland. They carried all manner of hunting supplies, including bows and arrows. Rob slowly perused the merchandise, paying particular attention to the arrows on display. None matched the arrow we had found.

Hoyt and Easton were two of the big brands at the time, but the one we found was a Bear. The markings on the shaft said "Bear/Jennings Realtree" and "2216," which indicated the length of the shaft. The arrow had a broadhead point that was screwed onto the shaft, enabling the point to be changed out, depending on what was being hunted.

The broadhead point was as sharp as a surgical tool and was designed to cause large wounds. It was used primarily when hunting large animals. Or humans. Rob thought it could be one of the new Bear Bruin points with a large 1.4-inch cutting diameter.

The shaft was made of aluminum. Solid carbon, which was more expensive than aluminum, was just starting to become popular in the mid-90s. The three rows of fletchings, or vanes, were made of two-inch-long plastic, a configuration preferred by hunters.

Rob went over to the glass counter to talk with the shop clerk. He pulled out a picture of the Bear arrow and asked the man behind the counter, "Do you know who carries Bear arrows like this in the area?"

"Well, now, let me think. That's not a brand we carry. Like the Eastons better myself. You could try down to Aim For It, out toward Capon Bridge. They might carry 'em. But I really think you'd be happier with the Eastons," said the man.

Rob drove the forty miles to Aim For It. The shop owner did not sell Bear arrows and did not know anyone in the area who did.

He worked his way through the list of other shops with no luck. The arrow supplier was another dead end.

After Rob left the first store, the guy behind the counter picked up the phone. "Hey, Curtis, it's Harry over at the Cumberland Outdoor shop. I'm callin' 'cause there was this here guy in the shop today with a picture of an arrow askin' questions."

"Okaaaayyyy," Curtis said, not sure where this conversation was leading.

"It was a Bear arrow. Looked kinda like the ones you picked up at the hunting show down in Virginia. Don't see many of them 'round here like that. When I saw the picture, I thought of you," said Harry.

"Why was this guy showing you a picture of an arrow?" asked Curtis.

"Not sure, he didn't say," said Harry.

"What did you tell him?" asked Curtis.

"I told him to go check on over to the Aim For It in Capon Springs," said Harry. "I knows he don't have no Bear arrows, but the guy didn't look like he was from around here, so I figured I'd send him huntin'."

"Good man," said Curtis. "What did this guy look like?"

"Heavy set, bearded, maybe in his late 60s. Kinda tall. Had a military set to him, he did," said Harry. "Acted like he knew somethin' 'bout bow huntin'."

Curtis didn't think that was anyone he knew. He'd ask around. "I appreciate the call," said Curtis and hung up the phone.

He sat for several minutes staring at the receiver. He went over to the cabinet where he stored his hunting bows and arrows. He remembered buying several arrows at the hunting conference in Virginia. Wanted to try out some of the new stuff, especially the carbon arrows that were supposed to be lighter and stronger than the aluminum. He didn't exactly remember what all he'd bought. He poured himself some whiskey and sat for a while longer, staring into the glass. Then he went back to the phone and made a call.

When the call was answered, Curtis said, "Did one of you two jackasses take an arrow from my cabinet?"

There was a longer-than-normal silence on the other end and some whispered conversation that Curtis could still hear.

"Shit man, it's Uncle Curtis," said one whispered voice. "He wants to know if we took one of his arrows."

"Fuckin' answer him, dude," said the second whispered voice.

Now in a regular tone of voice, the first voice said, "Hey, Uncle Curtis. Long time. We did see some cool arrows when we were at your house t'other day. We thought you wouldn't mind if we tried 'em out for target practice."

"Bring 'em back," Curtis ordered.

More whispering.

"Is that your brother there with you?" asked Curtis.

"Ah, yeah, he's here. He says that, ah, one of 'em broke first time we shot it so we done threw it out," said the voice.

"It was a piece of shit, and I wouldn't buy that kind no more if'n I was you."

"How many did you take?" asked Curtis. He took a long drink from his whiskey glass to keep from crawling down the phone line and strangling these two.

"A couple?" The voice answered in the form of a question, not really a statement.

"How many is a couple to you dumb shits?" asked Curtis.

More whispered conversation between the brothers.

"Two, but maybe three. Not rightly sure," said the voice.

"I want you both to think real hard right now. Was one of 'em a Bear?" asked Curtis.

"No, sir. We didn't shoot no bear. Just targets," said the voice.

"I am on my last nerve with you two. Bear is a brand name for an arrow," said Curtis. He slammed down his whiskey glass on the table, splashing whisky onto the table and all over his hand. He wiped his hand off on his jeans.

"Ohhh," said the voice. Whispers in the background. "Might could be."

"You need to listen to me closely, you idiots," said Curtis. "Until after the trial, I don't want either of you to touch a bow or an arrow, is that clear?"

"How we 'sposed to bring you back the arrows if'n we can't touch 'em?" said the voice.

Well, Curtis thought, *I guess they have a point.*

"I'll stop by tomorrow and git 'em myself," said Curtis. He slammed down the handset.

�֎

We decided that we would let it be known that I got shot with an arrow during the snowstorm. We were leaving out the part about my ass being on the receiving end.

A great opportunity presented itself on my next trip to the post office. It was like Grand Central Station. Six or seven people were milling about the lobby. A perfect audience for my story. As I was coming to the end of the story, our neighbor, Curtis, came into the post office. He walked up to the counter and the postmaster retrieved his mail and handed it to him. Curtis turned around to face the group, curious to see what everyone was talking about.

"Sam here was shot with an arrow during the snowstorm," said one of the neighbors to Curtis. "Now, I hear tell you're a big bow hunter, ain't you, Curtis? You didn't by accident shoot poor Sam while you was out deer huntin'?"

"Don't be ridiculous," said Curtis. "I was home in front of the fire with the wife and my huntin' dogs, where every sane person should've been during that storm. No offense, Sam."

Offense taken. Curtis nodded firmly as if that put an end to that discussion and promptly exited stage left.

Fred Weisman, another neighbor in my parents' subdivision, came up to me to chat. I knew who he was but had not had an opportunity to talk with him.

"Was wondering if I could ask a favor," said Fred.

Maybe he wants a wine cellar like Otto's, I thought.

"I'm kind of a Civil War buff," said Fred. That explained his white, curled handlebar mustache. Vintage Civil War.

He continued, "Would your parents mind if I walked their property with a metal detector? The Union Army was encamped outside of Paw Paw to guard the railroad. There were also encampments in and around Old Town and along the South Branch. I've found a few items on my property. I didn't have a chance to search that site before it was sold," said Fred. "I'd be happy to give them anything I find."

"I'll ask them, but I don't think they'll mind," I said. "I'll let you know."

When Curtis got back home from the post office, he felt the need for another whiskey in the middle of the day. He sat down in his oversized chair by the fireplace and picked up the phone. He held it for a few minutes before dialing the same number he had called the other day.

"Just got back from the post office," said Curtis.

"That's nice, Uncle Curtis. Did you get anything interesting in the mail?" said the voice.

"No, but I did hear an interesting story while I was there."

"Sure is a good place to catch up on the local news."

"I heard tell that one of 'em new city folks over to that new subdivision along the river got shot with an arrow during the snowstorm. You happen to know anything about that?"

"Can't say's I do," said the voice, but not very convincingly.

"If you do, I don't want to know nothin' 'bout it," said Curtis. "What I do want you to do is to go outside right now and build a good roarin' fire in the fire barrel. I'll be there in twenty minutes."

"Are you bringin' wieners and marshmallows?" said the voice. Snickering was heard in the background.

"You'll be lucky if it's not your wiener I'm roastin'," said Curtis.

When Curtis arrived, he ordered the two brothers to

bring him the arrows they had taken from his house. He inspected the arrows, but neither of them was a Bear. He placed the arrows in the burning barrel and stood there silently, watching them burn, melting the plastic and aluminum. The two brothers stood next to him, sending each other dagger looks.

"When this here fire's out, I want you to take the contents of the barrel and dump it in the river," said Curtis. "There's some guy with a picture of a Bear arrow. You better get down on your knees and pray to Jesus that's not my arrow and he doesn't track it back to you or me."

"But Uncle Curtis . . ." one of the brothers started.

"I don't want to hear nothin' you have to say," said Curtis. "Just nod if we understand each other."

The two brothers looked at each other, then reluctantly nodded their heads up and down.

Cherry brought us her first piece of information in response to the reward offer. One of her regulars told her about an urban legend among the locals that supervised workers who came in from outside the country to work at the TriCounty Labor Camp. At least one per year would go missing, and none of them ever came back. It was rumored that any men that left the camp without permission were eliminated by a sanctioned government enforcer.

Rob and Otto, both as you would expect pro-government, said the story was ridiculous. There were any number of reasons why they all didn't come back that didn't involve murder. They made their own way home. They got picked up by immigration and deported. They married a US citizen. But Rob and Otto also knew that sometimes the government could go to extremes.

Many of the men at the camp were of African American descent, possibly like Barrel. They told Cherry someone would investigate the story and let her know if it led to information pertinent to the dead bodies.

About a week later, Cherry received a second tip from another regular. She described him as a sweet old man with a tendency to overdo his medicinal marijuana—for the cancer, you know. He said people at the commune where he lived had reported seeing several spirits where the bodies were buried and that the place had a bad aura. He predicted that all the bodies had not been found yet. He offered to have one of the shamans come over to do a cleansing. Nothing useful to help identify the two bodies or who might have buried or unburied them.

Otto and Rob were beginning to question the merits of posting the reward, which so far had led to ghosts and government assassins.

Thirty days from move-in day, Anna and I were sealing the birch floors. I found a huge log for the other side of the stairs and was notching in the steps. We would set them in place in the next few days. All the cupboards and appliances were in.

On the way into town one day, I called my parents and told them about the neighbor's request to use a metal detector to search for Civil War artifacts. For them, it added to the charm of the place. They readily agreed. Not sure they would think the two dead bodies were charming. Or that it was charming their one and only son was shot in the ass with an arrow. That, I didn't tell them. But I was running out of time.

I stopped at Fred's house to tell him he could come over with his metal detector. He had a log home, too. It was stuffed with antiques and display cases with bullets and arrows and all manner of items that Fred had found over the years. He was a retired history teacher, and he explained every item to me. In minute detail. He could talk the ear off a dead sow, a colloquial expression I heard a local use. My mom was going to love this. I was more interested in his house. I told him he should come by any time. Still no phone. No need to call first. Anytime was fine. Yep, okay, got to go now.

Fred came by with his metal detector, a shovel, and an ancient beagle with white on his muzzle that waddled along beside him. Zoey and Zeus greeted both visitors with polite sniffs. Fred was wearing a vest with lots of pockets. He bent Anna's ear about Civil War history for a good half-hour. She kept asking him more and more questions. What a good sport. I was hiding upstairs.

When he came back several hours later, he pulled a couple of bullet fragments and a piece of cast iron shot from his pocket to show us. I think he was a little disappointed. He said that if there had been an encampment here, there would have been a lot of other finds.

He told us he found a pile of modern-looking tools that had been buried under some leaves. Those bad Z goldens. He also said that there may be a couple of metal tanks of some kind buried, maybe old oil tanks the farmers used. He said he marked the area with a flag. He dug down about twelve inches but didn't hit anything. He told us his metal detector could detect a large metal tank up to three feet down. Great. Potential ground contamination not disclosed at closing.

It was a beautiful spring-like evening, warm for that time of year. Otto and I had arranged to play tennis. I told Otto about Fred's visit.

"What if the tanks hold more bodies?" asked Otto. Huh, I didn't think about that.

"We have to dig them up then," I said. "Does Rob have a backhoe in his menagerie of man toys?"

"I don't think so," said Otto. "We could rent one."

"Sonny is coming back to finish putting stone on the fireplace. I know he has one. I'll ask him to bring it," I said.

"Should we alert Detective Wilson?" I asked.

"Good one," said Otto, but he meant the opposite. "Detective Wilson is not going to come out here to dig up some old tanks."

Otto still whupped my ass in tennis.

When Sonny arrived, I told him we were going to dig up some dead bodies. He was wise to my wisecracks, so he laughed good-naturedly.

"I'll be here workin' on the fireplace," said Sonny. "You let me know if you need any help."

I got to operate the backhoe. Finally! Both Rob and Otto were equipped with crowbars to remove any rocks that impeded our progress. About two feet down, the bucket hit something solid. I moved twelve inches to the right and struck something solid again. Another twelve inches, same thing.

Rob and Otto jumped into the pit and brushed away loose dirt. It was not a rock. Looked like metal. I widened the area of the hole to eight feet by eight feet by two feet deep. Two tanks were buried in the hole. They each had a hatch at the top. We needed to open them before we could move them. If there was still any fuel in the tank, there was a risk of explosion.

We used the crowbars to open the first rusted hatch. Inside the tank was more dirt, which was the proper way to decommission an old tank. It soaked up any residual oil or gas inside the tank. We opened the second tank. Same thing.

We all sat down on the edge of the hole, staring at the two tanks.

"Now what?" I asked.

"We should cut off the top and bring in the cadaver dogs," said Rob.

"How should we cut it off?" asked Otto.

Rob and I both said "acetylene torch" at the same time. Jinx. Because there didn't appear to be any oil or gas left, we wouldn't blow anything up or start ourselves on fire.

"Sam, have you got one?" Rob asked.

"Yeah, but not on me," I said.

"I'll go get mine," said Rob.

I didn't doubt it for a second.

Rob had both tops cut off in less than an hour. He had a face shield and special gloves that went up to his elbows.

Otto went to radio his FBI friends. If another body was found, the local authorities might involve the FBI in a serial killer investigation. The FBI cadaver dog and handler would come out tomorrow.

"So do we dig by hand or wait?" I asked.

"No sense in digging if these are just old tanks filled with dirt," said Otto. "Let's go have a drink, and we'll see what we see tomorrow."

We went back to Otto's place. I had a beer. Otto and Rob had some bourbon.

The FBI cadaver dog alerted positive. Otto called Detective Wilson and the FBI. He requested crime scene techs. We taped the area off. The FBI and county teams would arrive the next day.

It looked like an archeological dig. We sat in lawn chairs away from the action to watch. Multiple people equipped with brushes and small shovels slowly removed the dirt from the tanks. About eighteen inches deep into one tank, a technician found some slate pieces that appeared to have pictures etched into them. They were photographed, bagged and set aside. This first day, no bodies were discovered, but it was slow work.

The second day, the state police joined the search. Layer by layer of dirt was removed from the tanks. Some technicians were sifting the dirt for any additional clues. The top of bones began to appear in the dirt in both tanks. All of the techs switched to brushes only. More authorities arrived. The coroner was called. They found a silver charm bracelet. In the dirt under one of the bodies, they found many rhinestones made of glass. All that was left of both bodies were bones. Like Sally and Barrel, these bodies were not buried here recently.

Meanwhile, at the County Courthouse in Romney, the two males that may have been related to Curtis were convicted of cattle rustling and sentenced to ten years in prison. While they were being processed, it was determined that their fingerprints at booking were smudged, and they were re-fingerprinted before being remanded to the Hampshire County jail. The fingerprints triggered an alert to a case Detective Wilson was working on, but he was in the field. He didn't receive the alert until he returned two days later from the site on my parents' property with the two bodies buried in oil tanks.

Detective Wilson found the fingerprint alert in his pile of messages when he returned to the office. The prints belonged to Deacon and Dixon Johnson, recently convicted of stealing cattle. Deacon and Dixon Johnson were known to local authorities for causing trouble but always managed to elude charges. Their father, Huck Johnson, on the other hand, was currently serving a fifteen-year sentence at Martinsburg Correctional Center for assault and battery in connection with a bar fight that put a man in the hospital. Huck was arrested not long after his oldest son, Deacon, graduated from high school and shortly after Huck's wife passed. Custody of the younger son, Dixon, a junior in high school, was awarded to his uncle, Curtis Johnson. The prints matched partial prints recovered from the inside of the trunk of an old Cadillac where a body was found. Anna's car.

Deacon and Dixon's prints also pinged the FBI's database, and an alert was sent to Otto's FBI friend that printed a Bear arrow found in the woods.

Detective Wilson and an FBI agent who had been formally assigned to the case, Agent Harris, went to visit Deacon and

Dixon Johnson at the Hampshire County jail. Each brother was placed in a separate interview room.

Agent Harris was of average height, in his forties, with a receding hairline that looked like it might result in significant baldness in a couple of years. He had been with the FBI for going on twenty years. He knew a retired FBI employee had some connection with this case, but he did not know him personally. He specialized in serial killer investigations and had dozens of convictions under his belt throughout the US. He was skilled at de-escalating animosity with state and local police forces. He didn't know it, but Otto Rutherford had recommended to some people that Harris be assigned to the case.

Detective Wilson was quite happy to have his assistance. Hampshire County didn't have the time, the manpower, or the budget to identify the bodies that had been dead for over a decade. He also hoped that Agent Harris' involvement would insulate him from the pressure that the neighborhood residents, including the ex-FBI guy, Otto Rutherford, were putting on the investigation. Detective Wilson thought they would make a good team. He would handle the local yokels. Harris could handle everything else.

Detective Wilson and Agent Harris were able to observe the two Johnson brothers, both in their twenties. The younger, Dixon, was fidgety and nervous. His eyes darted back and forth. They decided to start with him.

Detective Wilson slid a picture of the old, decrepit Cadillac over to Dixon.

"Do you recognize this car, son?" asked Detective Wilson.

"Nuh, uh," said Dixon.

"Do you have any idea why your prints were found inside the trunk of this car?"

"Nope."

"Do you know what else we found inside the trunk of this car?"

"A tire?" said Dixon with a nervous shrug.

"No," said Wilson, "a dead body."

"Huh," said Dixon. His legs started jiggling under the table.

"Now you listen, son. You are already looking at ten years for stealing that cow. We have enough evidence with just your fingerprints to charge you as an accessory after the fact to murder, which could add twenty years or more to your sentence. You tell us everything you know about this body, and we'll see about getting your sentence reduced," said Agent Harris.

Detective Wilson slid another photo over to Dixon.

"Do you recognize this arrow?" said Detective Wilson.

"I'm no expert. They all look the same to me," said Dixon.

"Your prints were found on this arrow too."

"Go figure."

"This arrow was fired at two unarmed people in the middle of the last big snowstorm we had. One of them has an arrow wound. That's attempted murder that we can add to your growing list of charges."

"I didn't shoot nobody with no arrows."

"I'm guessing you might know who did, though."

Detective Wilson slid another picture over to Dixon.

Dixon winced when he looked at it and pushed it back to Detective Wilson.

"We found this partially buried body not far from the Cadillac with the dead body in the trunk," said Detective Wilson.

"Look, I don't know nothin' 'bout no dead bodies," said Dixon.

Another picture slid over to Dixon. Of the oil tank with the skeleton in it.

"And I suppose you don't know about this one either," said Detective Wilson. "Or this one." He pushed the picture of the fourth body to Dixon.

"These here skeletons look older than I am," said Dixon.

"But I am guessing you messed with at least two of them and probably know who killed them," said Agent Harris.

Detective Wilson slid a picture of one of the slate etchings toward Dixon. On it was carved a pixie. Dixon looked at it a long time. His eyes were not focused on the picture; it was like he was trying to remember something. It didn't come to him, but maybe it would.

"Nice artwork," said Dixon.

"One of the bodies was found with several of these rhinestones," said Agent Harris, and he slid a picture of what looked like diamonds mixed in with dirt.

"Bet they was stolen, then," said Dixon, nodding his head sagely to himself.

The last picture they showed Dixon was of a silver charm bracelet. It had little charms on it. Balloons and clowns and trapeze artists. When Dixon looked up from the picture, there was a flicker of fear in his eyes. He said nothing.

"If you tell us who did this, it will go a long way to getting you out of prison before you are a senior citizen. Our next stop is your brother, who's waiting for us in the next room. One or the other of you is going to give us the information, but only one of you is getting a deal," said Detective Wilson.

"You go on, talk to my brother. He don't know nothin' neither," said Dixon and sullenly slouched down in his seat, crossing his arms over his chest, his leg still bouncing nervously under the table.

When Agent Harris and Detective Wilson walked into the interrogation room where Deacon was waiting, his demeanor was completely different from his brother's. Where the brother was sullen and nervous, Deacon was confident, almost aggressive. The brothers were Irish twins, born twelve months apart. Deacon had all of the characteristics of the firstborn. They would take a different approach with Deacon.

"Just finished talking with your brother," said Detective Wilson. "He had some very interesting things to say about you."

"Why am I sittin' here?" asked Deacon.

"We need to talk with you about some dead bodies that were found out on the peninsula along the Potomac River."

"You fellas are wasting your time. I don't know nothin' about dead bodies."

"I think you do, and according to your brother, you dug one up and put it in an old Cadillac."

"He's a liar."

"We have both of your prints inside the trunk of the car and on the tarp wrapped around the body."

"If you know so much, then why ain't you arrestin' me?"

"Oh, we plan to charge you as an accessory after the fact to murder. Carries a sentence of twenty years, so you'll be sitting in prison at least three decades. But we could knock that down if you tell us who murdered the girl."

"No idea. Can't help you."

"We found three other bodies out in the woods near the car. Two were found in old oil tanks. Take a look at this picture."

They showed Deacon the picture of the charm bracelet with the clowns on it. He gave no reaction. Then they showed him the picture of the rhinestones. Deacon held that photo a bit longer than the one with the charms, and his face twitched before he rearranged it into a neutral expression. For a minute, it looked like anger. They let the silence stretch out. Then the two detectives stood up at the same time and walked out the door.

They went into a conference room and sat down.

"I don't think these boys killed these people," said Agent Harris.

"I agree, but I think they moved one of the bodies and tried to move the other," said Detective Wilson. "Either it was for family, or they got hired to do it."

"My team checked their bank account records. If someone hired them, they got paid in cash and didn't put it in the bank," said Agent Harris.

"There was some reaction to a couple of the pictures. Let's let the two of them discuss this among themselves and then bring them back in a couple of days. In the meantime, let's bring in their uncle, Curtis Johnson, and see what he knows," said Detective Wilson.

⚒

Every couple of weeks, Curtis went to visit his brother, Huck, at the prison. For this visit, they had a lot to discuss.

"Police found dead bodies down toward the river," said Curtis.

"That so," said Huck.

"Your sons were questioned in connection with the investigation."

"Those boys have always managed to get themselves into trouble. Don't strike me as killers, though."

"Did you ask them to dig up a body?"

"Now, why would I go and do that?"

"Oh, I don't know, maybe so those folks over in the new subdivision didn't find 'em."

Huck leaned forward and dropped his voice. "OK, I knew they was there. You know Pops was a bad seed. I was tryin' to protect the family name."

"Pops is dead, and what he did was a long time ago. If you had just left things as is, maybe it would never have been connected back to us. Now your sons are under suspicion, and I'm being called in for questioning."

"If the two idiot boys hadn't messed it up, it would have been fine."

"Why in the hell would they put a body in the trunk of some stranger's car?"

"They told me they was interrupted and panicked. They had just dug up one of the bodies and had started on the other. Guess they heard a noise in the woods. They moved the one body and stashed it in the trunk. They went back for it the next day in the middle of the night. By some crazy logic only their heads understand, they tried to take the car away with the body in it, but the car was so rusted the bumper fell off. Then they got arrested for that stupid cow stunt before they could go back and sort it out. That's when the cops found the bodies."

"Because of their stupidity, I'm now in the middle of this."

"Well, they did manage to move one of the bodies successfully."

"Wait a minute. The cops said they found four bodies. Are you tellin' me there were five bodies?"

"Far as I knew, there should only have been four."

"Somehow, I don't believe you."

"Blood is blood, brother. You gotta take care of this now."

"The police will probably question you, too. You do what you need to do to protect your sons."

Curtis went to the police station to meet with Detective Wilson and Agent Harris. They showed him the pictures of the bodies and the items found with them. They asked him where he was on the night the Cadillac was stolen. He said he was at home with his wife.

They showed him a picture of the arrow found the night Sam was shot. It was a struggle, but he kept his expression neutral. Target practice his ass. Those boys went and tried to shoot someone with his arrow. He said that he mostly used Easton arrows. He might at one time have had a Bear or two, but he didn't at present. They were welcome to come to look at his bow closet.

He had no firsthand knowledge of who moved the bodies or who killed them. The detectives felt that he knew more than he was saying. They told him not to leave town without letting them know. He said he had no plans to leave town.

The next day, Curtis went to visit Deacon and Dixon in jail.

"I talked with your Paw. How many, ah, parcels did he tell you to move?" asked Curtis.

"Four," said Deacon. "We messed up the first two, but the third went OK."

"And what did you do with the third parcel?"

"We done put it in the woodchipper. Then threw the pieces in the river."

"Did your Paw tell you who killed those people?"

"Naw, he just said we needed to do it to protect the family name."

"Boys, you listen here. Your granddad was a bad sort. Based on what your Paw told me, I believe he was responsible for those bodies. Our 'family name' is ruined what with what your Paw done and you two done already. I don't want to see you spend the rest of your lives in jail. If you have a chance to make a deal, you give up your granddad. It can't hurt him none now that he dead. And the rest of us'll be fine."

Dixon looked around the room to make sure no one was listening. "But here's the thing, Uncle Curtis. I don't think it was Granddad or only Granddad that killed all them people. The police, they showed me a picture of this charm bracelet with clowns on 'em. Paw brought this girl home from the circus to show us magic tricks when we was little. She had on a bracelet kind of like that one there. Then he said he drove her back to the circus."

"Lot of girls wore them kind of charm bracelets. That don't mean nothin'."

Deacon was silent and brooding through this exchange. He blurted out, "I think Paw kilt my prostitute."

"I'm gonna need some more context for that one, son," said Curtis.

"My graduation. I hired some prostitutes for the party. I'd just settled in with this cute little Asian chick and was about to get what I paid for when Paw showed up, bashed in the car window and drug the girl out by her hair," said Deacon.

"Then she disappeared and was never heard from again 'round here. Thing is, she had this sparkly dress on, kinda like them rhinestones I seen a picture of from the police. By my graduation, Granddad had passed on."

"I don't think the police know who those dead bodies are or when exactly they were murdered. You two hold out for a deal. Full immunity for both of you. Tell 'em your granddad did it. It'll protect you and your Paw, should he need protectin'," said Curtis.

The police and the FBI went to question Huck. His response to all of their questions was "I dunno." Except when he was asked if he or his sons killed anyone. He said no to that.

On his next regularly scheduled visit, Curtis laid out the plan for Huck. The boys would ask for full immunity and say that the bodies were killed by Pops. He asked Huck if he was okay with that. Huck nodded yes, okay.

When the detective and Agent Harris went back to interview the Johnson boys, the boys each separately told them they had some information that they could share, but they wanted full immunity for both of them. The detective and Agent Harris had kept track of the visitors to both the prison where Huck was incarcerated and the two brothers, so they knew the Johnson family had hatched some kind of plan. Didn't mean the plan would work, but any information might be helpful in a case that had very few clues. It would be hard to make the accessory after the fact charge stick, especially when the bodies had been dead for a decade or longer.

The boys were granted full immunity for that crime . . . but they didn't pay very close attention to what the full immunity covered. They thought they were ticking off the boxes of the plan Uncle Curtis laid out. Not the sharpest tools in the toolbox.

Deacon and Dixon told the detectives that their granddad was responsible for the bodies they dug up.

"How do you know?" Detective Wilson asked Dixon.

"Ahh, well, you see, we all knew Granddad wasn't right in the head. I think it was my Paw, yeah, it was my Paw that told me Granddad was bad and had kilt some folks. Buried 'em a ways off on the neighbor property," said Dixon. Detective Wilson and Agent Harris nodded their heads yes, as if they believed every word of that obvious lie.

When they asked Deacon, he said: "Granddad tole me one night when he was stinkin' drunk just afore he passed. He tole me where he buried 'em and that I should make sure no one ever found 'em."

"And how many bodies did he say he killed?" asked Agent Harris.

"He dint," said Deacon.

"When your grandfather made this confession to you, did he tell you who the bodies were?" asked Detective Wilson.

"Naw," said Deacon. "At the time, I thought he was just drunk and tellin' stories. It wasn't 'til them new neighbors moved in, and I started worryin' about it that Dixon and I went to check. Took us some diggin' to find them two."

"What about the two bodies in the oil tanks?" asked Agent Harris.

"It's not like he gave me a list of who and where," said Deacon. "We found the two and got interrupted. Then we's got arrested and couldn't look no more. Honest, we didn't think there would be five bodies."

"How many bodies?" asked Agent Harris.

"Wait, what?" said Deacon. "What I say?"

"You said five bodies," said Detective Wilson.

"Tha's what you told me, right? Five bodies," said Deacon.

"No, we said four," said Detective Wilson.

"Got a few things going on in here right now. Hard to keep track," said Deacon.

The two officers nodded their heads up and down like they believed this story. Now they were looking for a fifth body.

✗

Wilson and Harris left the prison and drove over to see Huck again.

"When Pops was drinkin' whiskey, he'd wax on about keepin' his community free from outsiders. He used to tell these stories 'bout how he helped by gettin' rid of any he come across. I never knew for sure whether he was makin' it up," said Huck. "I do remember this one time when I was a kid. We picked up this Black guy at a diner in Cumberland. He had a funny accent. Not from America. Anyways, Pops offered to drive this guy somewhere. Instead, Pops stopped in the woods. He and that guy walked off, left me sittin' in the truck. Just Pops came back. Pops told me he got him where he needed to go. There was this kind of weird vibe I got from Pops, but I didn't think on it 'til just now."

It was clear to the detectives that the Johnson family had sewn up their little plan. Now they were going to pick it apart.

They started with a search warrant for the residence where the Johnson boys lived before their arrest, which was in the family home where Huck and Curtis grew up with their father. Huck and Curtis's mother had passed away of cancer several years ago. Their father died in 1987 of a heart attack.

The team was looking for any evidence of a murder that occurred at the home or around the property and anything else that might connect the Johnson family to the murders of four or five bodies. Cadaver dogs were brought in to search the house and property, too.

The cadaver dogs alerted on the woodchipper, but no blood was found in or around the machine. No blood was found in the home or in any of the outbuildings. The cadaver dogs alerted again on a canoe that was upside down on a rack next to one of the sheds.

When they searched the outbuildings, they found some old women's clothes and items in boxes. These were sent to the FBI crime lab for inventorying and analysis. They could be old items of Huck's and Curtis's mother or Huck's wife. They also removed an old hunting rifle that hung over the fireplace.

Most of the contents of the house appeared to be recent junk belonging to Deacon and Dixon. They confis-cated a hunting bow found in a closet. There was a pile of straw bales with targets on them at the back of the build-ings that looked like a shooting range for guns and bows.

⚒

While the interviews and the search of the Johnson family farm were going on, the FBI was running some of the items found with the bodies through their missing persons database, which was more comprehensive than the one maintained by the state police. They got a hit on the slate etching of a pixie. A girl named Brenda Rafferty went missing in 1980. She was last seen in Maine but was believed to be heading to West Virginia. The exact location of her disappearance was unknown. She was believed to be carrying some slate etchings with her when she disappeared. Mr. and Mrs. Rafferty lived in Ohio and continued to put out bulletins and announcements to try to find Brenda.

Agent Harris, on the FBI's budget, flew to Ohio to interview Mr. and Mrs. Rafferty. When he called ahead to let them know he was coming, he said he wanted to ask them some questions about Brenda's disappearance. When he met with them, he showed them a picture of the pixie etching that had been found in the oil drum in West Virginia. Mrs. Rafferty looked at the picture and started to cry. She said it was Brenda's. Agent Harris obtained Brenda's dental records while he was in Ohio. They matched the body found in Anna's old Cadillac.

The charm bracelet was included in the description of a girl who disappeared in 1981 from Cumberland, Maryland. Hilda Abernathy was a clown actress for the Hubler International Circus. She went into town to buy a scarf and never returned to work. Her parents, Elsa and Axel Abernathy, lived in Wisconsin. Agent Harris continued west from Ohio to

Wisconsin to meet with them. When Mrs. Abernathy saw the charm bracelet, she fainted and had to be revived with smelling salts. Agent Harris pulled the dental records for Hillie, as her parents said she was called. Her dental records did not match any of the four bodies that had been recovered in West Virginia. Agent Harris also borrowed several pictures of Hillie taken while she was performing. She was happy and vivacious, interacting with the audience.

One item found in the boxes of women's items taken from the Johnson farm was a silky red scarf. It still had the sales tag on it and listed the store as GC Murphy in Cumberland, Maryland. Agent Harris read through the detective's files from when Hillie disappeared. He noted that they had interviewed a store clerk at GC Murphy who remembered selling a red scarf to Hillie. There were also pictures of Hillie performing a magic trick that Agent Harris had collected from Hillie's parents. Her hand was at the side of a woman's head, and it looked like she was pulling a red scarf out of the woman's ear.

Fingerprinting the scarf was negative for prints, which was not unexpected. Fingerprints only lasted on clothing for a couple of years.

The crime techs were unable to lift any prints off the bracelet, which had been buried for fifteen years in the dirt-filled oil tank. This could perhaps be the fifth missing body that Deacon had let slip was murdered by his grandfather or possibly someone else.

�֎

One day after the search warrant was executed on the Johnson farm, Agent Harris, with the caravan of FBI vehicles, drove up my parents' driveway. I hailed Otto and Rob on the shortwave radio. They rode over in Rob's Hummer. Agent Harris gave us all a report of what they had found so far. He said that Deacon and Dixon Johnson had confessed to moving two bodies in exchange for immunity and that they believed their grandfather, now deceased, killed the people buried in the woods. He told us they had identified Sally, the body found in Anna's trunk, whose name was Brenda Rafferty from Ohio. The investigation of how Brenda's body was connected to the deceased Johnson was ongoing. He also said that another woman, Hilda Abernathy, may have owned the charm bracelet that was found, but her body was not identified among the four already discovered. They had evidence that there might be a fifth body. Therefore, they wanted to do another search of my parents' property.

The Z goldens could hear the search dogs the FBI had brought. We made sure Zoey and Zeus were in the house tucked up tight with a couple of my tools and some dog toys to chew on so as not to interfere with the investigation. I was pleased in a way to know that there was more evidence discovered in the cases. If the murderer was dead, and all the bodies were out in the open, Anna and I, and my parents, should no longer be in danger.

"Did the Darryls, I mean the Johnsons, confess to shooting me in the ass?" I asked Agent Harris. Deacon and Dixon, Darryl and Darryl. I was not too far off.

"I am afraid not, Sam," he said. "That arrow did not have any blood on it, so it could not have been the arrow that shot you. It could have been shot at any time. I have no way to tie it to the Johnsons or anyone else at this time."

Like our search parties that Otto organized, the FBI team

formed a line and walked the entire property, but much slower than we did. The search dogs did not find any more bodies, and no further evidence was found.

Otto told Agent Harris about the boaters we heard the night of the ice storm.

"It could have been Deacon and Dixon moving the third body that day," said Otto.

"Did you see them?" asked Agent Harris.

We did not.

"Would you recognize their voices?" asked Agent Harris.

Maybe, we all agreed. It was worth a shot.

Otto, Rob, and I went to the police station in Romney for the voice ID. We were each in a different room, listening to voice recordings. The phrase spoken by each of the four speakers was the same: "No one is going to be out in this storm, you ass wipe." All three of us remembered hearing it the day of the ice storm. We compared notes after. Otto was sure it was number 2. Rob and I were not sure. The voice ID was inconclusive.

The FBI knew about the tip from an unidentified source about the missing TriCounty Labor Camp workers. It was a while before those records came in. For the twenty years from 1960 to 1980, about twenty-five men that started working at the camp left and did not return in the middle of the contract. None of them were ever officially reported missing to law enforcement. By searching immigration records, FBI investigators found that seven of them were subsequently detained and deported. Five of them were deceased. That left thirteen men that might be Barrel, the African American man left partially unburied by the Johnson boys.

The coroner had identified a healed-over fracture on the right forearm of Barrel. It was likely from an injury in childhood.

No living relatives could be identified for four of the thirteen missing men from the TriCounty Labor Camp. One of the men on the list had named his mother as next of kin, Laticia Ramoon, living in the Cayman Islands.

It was more than twenty years since Mrs. Ramoon had received the letter from the US government telling her that they did not know where her son was. Her husband had passed away, and all her children were grown and living their own lives. She was surrounded by grandchildren, but she often thought of her son, Anton. When the FBI caseworker called her to ask about her son, she couldn't believe it was real. The agent asked her if her son had had any injuries when he was a child. She had to think for a minute. She had seven rambunctious children and they did hurt themselves, like active children do. Anton was always in the trees. She used to call him her little monkey. She remembered he had fallen out of the tree when he was five or six and broken his right arm.

"Do you have any dental records for your son?" asked the agent. Her son had never been to see a dentist before he left the Cayman Islands. None of her children had been to a dentist when they were young.

"Did he have his arm X-rayed when he broke it?" asked the agent.

"With seven children, we were poor and couldn't afford doctors," said Mrs. Ramoon. "My neighbor was a nurse. She set the bone, and we used a board wrapped to his arm to keep it straight until the bone could heal. We made a sling out of some rags. Does this mean you found my son?"

"I am sorry, ma'am, it is an ongoing investigation. Your son has been missing for over two decades. We may never find him," said the agent. "An agent will follow up with you if we have any additional information."

The investigators asked Curtis to come back to the police station. They showed him pictures of Anton, Hillie, and Brenda and asked him if he recognized any of them. He honestly did not and told them so. They believed him. They showed the same pictures to Deacon and Dixon. Same "no" answers. They asked them if they had ever been to the circus with their father or their grandfather. Sure, lots of times, they said. Almost every year. Not much to do in this backwater town. Sometimes their father or their grandfather or both would take them. Deacon said Dixon loved the circus. Deacon thought it was stupid but better than sitting at home playing spit and catch.

The next day, they showed the pictures to Huck. When he looked at Brenda's and Hillie's pictures, he made a big showing of bringing them closer and then moving them farther away, like he was nearsighted. When he picked up Anton's photo, he said, "I dunno, all these folks look the same to me. Might could be the man my Pops drove. Might not," said Huck.

The investigation was running out of leads. Detective Wilson and Agent Harris asked Otto if he could talk to the "concerned citizen" that offered the reward for information. The investigators wanted to put out an official request to the public and state that a reward for information would be paid. Otto said he would ask. He called the next day and said that the concerned citizen, who did not wish to be named, had agreed. This concerned citizen had given Otto the money in cash, and he would bring it by the station.

Four official bulletins went out. Three with pictures— Anton, Hillie, and Brenda. Naming a $1,000 reward for information in connection with their disappearance. The fourth just had a description of a four-foot, nine-inch woman of Asian descent who may have gone missing sometime between 1985 and 1990 who may or may not have been wearing a rhinestone dress.

Cherry saw the announcements and called Otto. She told him that it would be very rare to see an Asian woman in this area of West Virginia at that time, especially one wearing a fancy dress with rhinestones. Unless, of course, she was a prostitute or exotic dancer. There were not many strip clubs other than Scruze and Dover in the area, but she did remember one that opened for a short time in the late 1980s over near Berkeley Springs. It wasn't open for very long. She didn't want to call the police and get involved. She asked if Otto would convey the information. Otto called Agent Harris and gave him the information.

One of the best places to get more information about a strip club was from the competitors. Agent Harris and Detective Wilson went to Dover first. It was early in the day. A couple of family members were there. They remembered a club that was around for a short while but then closed. Couldn't remember the name and didn't have any info about who owned it or worked there.

Next stop was Scruze. Cherry and a couple of the girls were there early, setting up for the after-work rush. Cherry had disappeared into the back. One young girl had just turned eighteen and was too young to remember a strip club five or more years ago. The other woman did remember.

"Yeah, I remember the place. I don't think they was open more than a year. Had a funny name like 'drive-in' or something. Not quite, but it had something to do with a car," said the woman. "It was owned by this giant of a woman. I saw her one time. She could almost be a man."

"Do you know her name?" asked Detective Wilson.

"Sure don't," said the woman.

"Anyone else here?" asked Detective Wilson.

"I think Cherry's still here in the back," said the woman. She yelled for Cherry.

The investigators asked if Cherry remembered the name of the club.

"I think it was called the Kiss 'N Ride," said Cherry.

"Did you know the owner's name?" asked Detective Wilson.

"No, sorry."

"Did you know anyone that worked there?"

"Nuh, uh."

A search of the county records turned up the Kiss 'N Ride Strip Club. It was registered to one Adoni Largess. Probably a stage name. Agent Harris sent the info to the FBI team for follow-up. A woman by the name of Adoni Largess, born Lisa Smith, was located. Currently living in Clearwater, Florida. Agent Harris hopped on a plane and went to visit her.

Agent Harris arrived at Ms. Largess's modest one-story house around 3 p.m. Ms. Largess answered the door in fuzzy high-heeled slippers and a bathrobe that barely covered the essentials. She towered over Agent Harris. He explained that they were working to identify some bodies found near Paw Paw, West Virginia. He asked her if she had any employees who may have gone missing from 1985 to 1990. She said she had employees leave without giving notice all the time.

"This employee would have been around four foot nine, possibly of Asian descent," said Agent Harris.

"Most of our Asian dancers are small. Could be a couple like that during that time period. Let me look back in the records. Can I let you know in a few days?"

"Do you have pictures of your dancers in their personnel files?"

"Yes, we do."

"Any chance you could look tomorrow? I'll stay overnight and wait if there is a chance I could get a photo."

"The right motivation sure could help things along."

Agent Harris pulled out five twenty-dollar bills. Ms. Largess said, "I'll see what I can do."

He gave her the name of the local Holiday Inn.

Ms. Largess called Agent Harris around 5 p.m. the next day. She had two employees matching his description. He went by her house to pick up the files.

Ms. Largess came to the door wearing a brightly patterned muumuu. Her big hair was hidden under a turban. She invited Agent Harris in, and he sat down on the sofa in the living room. One of the files she handed him was for a woman named Jae Pham. In the file was a picture of her wearing a silvery dress covered in rhinestones.

"This one, Jae Pham, do you remember what she was doing before she left?" said Agent Harris. "Says here her last day worked was June 17, 1989."

"That one was trouble from the very beginning. She would tell the customers she was here in the US against her will and wanted to return home to wherever she was from in Asia. She conned at least a dozen customers into buying her a plane ticket. She mostly worked private functions. I suppose I could see if I could find my calendar and see what job we had booked then." She sat there looking expectantly at Agent Harris, not moving.

He reached into his pocket, pulled out his wallet, and counted out five twenties again. "Do you think you could do that now?"

She accepted the bills, and they disappeared between her cleavage. "Of course, sugar. Just you wait right here."

Agent Harris waited until Ms. Largess left the room before he rolled his eyes.

Ms. Largess came back and sat down in a huff. "Yeah, I remember this now. She was booked for some private party out toward Paw Paw, West Virginia. Didn't show up for work the next day. I drove out to the place out on River Road near the river to see if I could track her down. Turns out it was some old, abandoned barn. There were a bunch of kids hanging around cleaning up the mess. Some high school kid booked the party. Told me Jae wasn't feeling well, and someone from the party drove her home. Never heard from her again. Then our place got shut down by the local goody two shoes, and we all left for greener pastures."

"Remember what this kid looked like?"

"Just your average kid. Nothing remarkable. Not too tall, not too fat. Just a kid."

"Glasses, tattoos, scars, facial hair, anything?"

"Nope, just your average white kid."

Agent Harris called Detective Wilson. Asked him to take a drive out to River Road and see if he could find an abandoned barn near the river. Five years later, it might have been taken down, but it might still be there. Fifty/fifty shot, he figured. Detective Wilson found only one old barn on River Road. It was still standing. A search and rescue dog searched the property while Agent Harris flew back to West Virginia.

No bodies were found at the site. Looked like it was a favorite party site for years, though. There was junk and trash everywhere. They taped it off. The techs came the next day to bag and tag all the garbage. In June, a party with high school kids could be a graduation party. Detective Wilson's neighbor had a son who graduated about five years ago. He'd ask the boy if he knew of a party out that way.

He waited until he saw his neighbor's son, Carson, return from work. Saw his car pull into the driveway.

He walked over.

"Could I ask you a quick question?" said Detective Wilson to Carson.

"Sure, what can I do you for?" said Carson.

"When did you graduate?"

"In 1989, sir."

"You can call me Chris. By any chance, do you remember hearing about a graduation party out in an abandoned barn on River Road?"

"Am I gonna get in trouble?"

"No, no, nothing like that. It's just background in an investigation."

"What, like a murder or something?"

"Ah, the investigation is ongoing. I'm not at liberty to say."

"Wow, I've never provided background in an investigation before."

"About that party . . ."

"Yeah, right. The Johnson kid threw a huge graduation party out at some barn. I didn't go, but I heard he had alcohol and even paid for some dancers to come in and dance and whatever. I also heard his father stirred up some kind of ruckus with one of the strippers."

"Deacon Johnson? Do you have some names of people who did go to the party?"

"Could they get in trouble?"

"I don't think so. Just more background, that's all."

"Okay, I'll write down some names and bring it 'round tomorrow."

✗

Wilson and Harris drove out to the prison again to talk with Deacon. They let him sit alone in the interview room for a good forty-five minutes.

Agent Harris went in first, alone.

He slammed the picture of Jae down on the table in front of Deacon and shouted, "You killed this girl, didn't you?"

Deacon jumped and blurted, "No, no, I didn't kill her. She was very much alive last time I saw her." Then he realized his mistake. His mouth formed a thin line, determined not to say another word.

Detective Wilson came in. He slammed another picture down next to the picture of Jae. It was the one of the skeleton found in one of the oil tanks.

"We found her remains out where you were digging up bodies," said Detective Wilson. "I have a dozen witnesses who saw you with her at your graduation party." Well, maybe not yet, but he would. "You killed her. Just make it easy on yourself and tell us what happened."

"I dint kill no one," said Deacon. "That's all I'm gonna say."

And that was all he did say.

Through interviews with the dozen or so witnesses who attended the party, the investigators learned that Deacon and Jae had driven off down the street a few hundred yards to be alone. Deacon's father showed up and smashed the car window, pulling Jae out by her hair. Deacon returned to the party alone, then left by himself. Last anyone saw, Jae went off with Deacon's father.

So Huck might be the last person to see Jae alive. And Huck's father couldn't have killed this woman because he was already dead.

The investigators went back to the other jail to interview Huck. Agent Harris carefully set the pictures of Jae wearing her sparkling dress and the skeleton on the table in front of Huck. A slight look of disgust passed across Huck's face.

"Just want to let you know we are charging your son Deacon in the murder of Jae Pham," said Detective Harris. "He hired her to dance at his graduation party. We have more than a dozen witnesses that saw them together. He is also a suspect in another murder of a person whose human remains were found in and around a woodchipper and a canoe at Deacon's property."

"That boy too stupid to kill somebody," said Huck. "He didn't kill no stripper. And y'all gave my sons immunity on moving the bodies my Pops done murdered. They prob'ly moved one of 'em in the canoe."

Bingo, confirmation of the fifth body.

"Were you with this girl that night?" asked Agent Harris.

"I heard about the party and went to check to make sure everything was on the up and up. You know, no drugs, that kinda thing. I found my son about to get a blow job from that girl and didn't think he needed to pay for it. There's nothin' wrong with the boy. He should be able to get that for free. I put a stop to that right quick," said Huck.

"You didn't take that girl off and get some action for yourself, did you?" asked Detective Wilson.

"Hell, no. Them Asian chicks not my type," said Huck.

"Some kind of father that would make you, to let your son go down for something you did," said Detective Wilson.

THE BIG MOVE

Move: (a) to change residence or location;
(b) to proceed in a particular direction;
(c) to take action.

I asked my wife if we had any more moving boxes.
She said we only have still boxes.
We bought them at a stationary store.

March 1995

While my parents undertook the painful process of getting ready to move from a house they had lived in for over thirty years, more progress was being made on the case. Deacon was charged with the murder of Jae Pham.

By the time of Curtis's next visit to Huck in prison, he had learned his nephew was charged with the murder of the stripper. Curtis was so mad he could hardly see straight.

"Did you have anything to do with the death of that stripper?" Curtis hissed to Huck across the table.

"It was an accident, man. She offered to perform a service since I interrupted her with Deacon. She was crazy kinky and wanted me to do this fixation thing," said Huck. He was getting a blank look from Curtis. "You know, where you choke her while she came. Said she couldn't without it, so I did."

"You mean erotic asphyxiation," said Curtis.

"If you say so," said Huck.

"You cannot let your son take the fall for this. You got to tell 'em what you told me. That it was an accident. If you don't and your son goes away for this, I will make your life a living hell. You will wish you were dead."

"OK, OK, I'll tell 'em."

"And let me understand this: she died, and you buried her in an oil tank?"

"Yeah, Pops stuck the bodies in the ground where anything could find 'em, dig 'em up. I didn't want her to be found. Some Chinese foreigner preying on our young. Pops got smarter toward the end, and he buried his last one in a tank. Thought it was a good idea."

Huck passed a message from the jail to Detective Wilson that he wanted to talk. He confessed his accident with Jae to the Detective. The Detective charged him with involuntary manslaughter, which carried a sentence of not more than one year, and concealment of a deceased human body, which carried a sentence of one to five years.

Based on his father's statement about the canoe, Deacon was also charged with concealment of a deceased human body. The charge was not likely to stick since no body was ever found. Deacon protested that he had immunity. The investigators corrected him. He had immunity for moving the one body found in the Cadillac and the second body partially unearthed. Not the third body Deacon had failed to disclose.

Agent Harris briefed Otto, who in turn briefed Anna and me on all of these events.

Anna and I drove back to Michigan to help my parents pack. Sonny was putting the finishing touches on the fireplace, a towering two-story masterpiece of local river rock that we pulled ourselves out of the river. He would keep an eye on things. Otto stopped by the house every couple of days.

When we arrived in Michigan, we told my parents the story of the bodies and everything that transpired while we were building the house. Zeus and Zoey lay between them on their feet to bring comfort. We watched my parents work through several stages of grief. First denial. This couldn't have happened. Then anger. How dare these people stain their land with their crimes. Then bargaining. Maybe we should sell the house, not live there. Then depression. What did we do? We thought we would be safe in the country. Then acceptance. What's in the past is passed. We will retake the property and make it a happy place.

Anna and I told them we would stay with them for a couple of months after the move to make sure they felt safe. If not, we could sell the house. Find or build another. It was just a house.

Anna and I promised each other we would never live in one house for more than five years. The amount of stuff my parents accumulated in the thirty years they lived in their house in Michigan was mind-boggling. We wanted to leave a couple of days before the movers arrived so that we could get back to the log home and do a thorough cleaning, but there was just too much packing to do. We ended up in a big caravan. My parents' two cars and my van. The movers made their own way.

When we got to the log home, all the lights were on, shining through the woods. Sonny was there waiting for us, and he threw open the front door.

"Welcome, welcome, Mr. and Mrs. Bradley," said Sonny.

My parents were exhausted. It was a long drive from Michigan. We worked long days getting ready with the packing and the moving. Yvonne looked around, and tears welled up in her eyes. We had warned her there would be a bit of dust and things to clean up, which Anna and I promised we would do before the movers came the next day with the furniture.

She excused herself and went to the basement. Nick patted Sonny on the arm and said, "It was a long day." He followed Yvonne into the basement.

Sonny sat down on the bottom step of the stairs and said, "She hates it, doesn't she?"

"What, the house?" I asked.

"No, the fireplace," said Sonny.

"Naw, man, it's not the fireplace. More likely, it's the dust and stuff we didn't get a chance to clean up before we left," I said. "I promise you, dude, she loves the fireplace. It's spectacular."

A few minutes later, Yvonne came back upstairs. She went to Sonny and gave him a great big hug.

"The fireplace is stunning. I have never seen anything like it," she said. Sonny was sunny again.

"I can't believe you didn't clean up before you left," she said to me. I looked appropriately ashamed. Anna could give me a spanking later.

The rest of the move-in was drama-free. The majority of the boxes were unpacked within a week. What wasn't unpacked was tucked away in a storage room in the basement. Anna and I had planned a surprise housewarming party thirty days after they arrived with the help of Otto and Regina. Scruze did not do the catering for this one. It was all highbrow with heavy hors d'ouevres that, to me, were not heavy at all. Little platters of tiny sandwiches that you could eat in one bite. Regina assured me she knew what she was doing.

On the day of the party, we sent Yvonne and Nick off on some ridiculous errand in Cumberland so we could get set up.

Anna and Regina had a multi-page honey-do list for me. As I worked my way through the list, I happened to glance out the living room French doors and noticed what looked like Rob's Hummer in the field across the river. The river was running low, so he could have driven across at the ford. I could see him moving around on the other side of his vehicle. As a distraction from the tedium, I imagined all the things he could be doing. Setting rabbit traps. Picking wild strawberries. At least he didn't have a honey-do list.

The evening of the party, the house glowed in natural light. Candles adorned almost every flat surface, and a fire danced in the fireplace. We kept the electric lights to a minimum. We hired a piano player who played classical music.

We invited all of the neighbors on the peninsula and those we met during our escapades. It was truly a celebration of life and new beginnings.

We even invited the shaman from the commune. To the delight of all of the guests, he declared the property and the house free of any bad spirits or auras.

We held a moment of silence to remember Brenda, Jae, and the two or three other bodies whose identities were not conclusively known. And their families and the families of all the missing who have to live every day not knowing what had happened to their loved ones.

I saw Rob across the room, and I went over to say hello.

"Saw you out across the river this afternoon," I said.

"Did you now," said Rob.

"Rabbit season ended a couple of months ago, right?" I said.

"I think so," said Rob. "Why do you ask?"

"Just wondering what you were doing," I said.

"Ah, I can't say," said Rob. "If you will excuse me . . ." Rob drifted off into the crowd of neighbors.

I had to say, the vague reply was very Rob-esque, but

now my imagination was working overtime. Had to put it on hold, though, because at that moment, Otto approached.

At my insistence, Otto had invited some of his friends to the party. I knew my parents would love meeting Otto's very cosmopolitan friends. He said there were a couple of people I needed to meet. Lyle Kilpatrick and his wife, Tabitha, were two of those people. Like Otto, Lyle was retired FBI. Job title undisclosed. They had purchased a one-hundred-acre farm outside of San Francisco.

"This home should be featured in a magazine," said Tabitha. "And we love the wine cellar you built for Otto."

"We wanted to know if you would be available to build a custom post and beam house overlooking the Pacific Ocean," said Lyle.

I said, "Yes, when should I start?" No, I said I would have to talk it over with Anna and let them know.

Just then, there was a loud explosion and a burst of light. This triggered a rush of adrenaline for yours truly. Another meteor? My head swiveled back and forth for a couple of seconds to locate the source, and then I heard it. A collective "ahh!" from the assembled group. A distinctive "ahh." A pleasurable "ahh." Almost exclusively heard from a group of people viewing . . .

Fireworks. Everyone was heading for the front porch. Right over the river, timed almost exactly thirty seconds apart, was a professional pyrotechnics display that only my buddy Rob could be responsible for. That's what he was doing in the field earlier.

Based on my years of firefighting experience, it looked like he had rigged a chain fuse, which you only had to light once. Then it ignited each firework, moving down the line.

He probably had them all loaded into wood frames. The first was probably a common rocket firework. It shot high and made a loud bang. The others were a mix of different styles. There were peonies and chrysanthemums, which created colorful globe-shaped displays like the flowers. There were willows, which left behind long trails of smoke from a central star that looked like the canopy of a willow tree. He had screamers and sizzlers, too. Ah, men and their toys.

Anna came up to me and took my hand. We stood and watched the light show together. I worried for just a second about whether I should get the hose out and start wetting down the roof. But she leaned her head on my shoulder, and I figured I could cross that bridge if it came to it. When it was all done, the clapping died down, and the roof did not catch fire, I turned to her and said, "Honey, see that couple over there? They are friends of Otto's. They would like to know if I could build them a house in California overlooking the Pacific Ocean."

"When can we start?" she said.

EPILOGUE

In 2004, the Forensic Science Center at Marshall University in Huntington, West Virginia, performed DNA testing on the two unidentified bodies found in the woods of Northeast West Virginia outside Paw Paw and the Johnson's woodchipper.

With familial DNA from Anton's youngest sibling against bones from the partially unearthed skeleton that we called Barrel, the results confirmed that the body was, in fact, Anton Ramoon, the young man who came from the Cayman Islands to work at the TriCounty Labor Camp to pick apples in the fall of 1970. The cause of death was marked inconclusive. No one was ever arrested in connection with his disappearance. The $1,000 reward was paid by the Hampshire County Police to Cherry's informer.

Hillie Abernathy's parents maintained her room as a shrine since her disappearance. Investigators retrieved hair that still had follicles attached to it from her hairbrush and were successful in matching the DNA from the hair to traces of bone dust recovered from the woodchipper at Deacon and Dixon's property. Deacon and Dixon, who had recently been released from jail after serving their sentence for stealing the cow, were charged with and convicted of concealment of a deceased human body and returned to jail to serve another five years. Her case remains an open cold case.

The DNA testing on the bones of the third body found in one of the oil tanks was added to the FBI's CODIS national DNA database. It didn't have any matches, but perhaps it would match someone in the future.

AUTHOR'S NOTES

Building a Log Home. My brother and I built my parents a log home in West Virginia in the 1990s. It wasn't far from Paw Paw. Sam's character was inspired by my brother, who is much funnier than Sam. He had two golden retriever puppies named Hercules and Venus. Other little tidbits of our experiences were woven into this fictional story and generally greatly exaggerated. Check out my Facebook page to learn more about those real-life experiences.

Granot Loma is a real 20,000-square-foot, fifty-room log home in the Upper Peninsula of Michigan. It sold for $4.5 million in 1987, according to news reports. It was built by an American businessman named Louis Kaufman in 1919 as a summer residence for his family. He named it by taking random letters from his wife's and children's names. Tom Baldwin, a bond trader, bought it in 1987 and had it completely restored. It is listed today as a National Historic Landmark.

TriCounty Labor Camp was a real place in Berkeley County, WV. It housed the apple pickers who were contracted under the federal government program called the British West Indies Program. The camp was operational from 1953 until 1992, when the bulk of the apple harvest workforce transitioned to Hispanic migrant workers.

Hubler International Circus was an actual circus owned by George Hubler (1922-2007) and based in Ohio. It included the Shrine Circus. According to historical schedules, the circus was, in fact, in Cumberland, MD, in July 1981.

Clown Classes. At the beginning of 1980, the University of Wisconsin-La Crosse began offering evening continuing education clown classes taught by Dr. Richard Snowberg. It became known as "Clown Camp" in 1981, with thirty-five people in attendance. Enrollment increased to more than three hundred by 2005. It continues to this day.

The Nightmare Before Christmas was an animated movie released in 1993. Two of the characters in the movie were named Sally and Barrel.

The Bob Newhart Show was a comedy show featuring comedian Bob Newhart. In September 1987, an episode titled "Prima Darryl" aired featuring the two brothers, both named Darryl.

GC Murphy, a discount department store, operated from 1906 to 2002. They had a store in Cumberland, MD.

Rainbow Gathering is a real event that takes place every year in July at different national parks throughout the country. It was held in West Virginia in 1981, which was the year two women that hitchhiked from Iowa were found dead. There have been several missing persons and deaths connected to the event over the years.

"Rainbow Girls" was the name the press gave to the two women from Iowa who were found murdered in 1981. A local man was tried and convicted of their murders, Jacob Beard, but was acquitted in 2000. The murders of the two women were never solved. The Rainbow murders have been the subject of a book written by Emma Copley Eisenberg and an A&E special.

The bridge at Old Town, MD is a one-lane, low-water bridge. It is one of the few private toll bridges in the United States. It is an all-wood bridge supported by concrete pedestals connecting West Virginia and Maryland that was built in 1937. It was sold to the Walters family in 1970, who operated the bridge until 1994, when it was closed due to damage from Hurricane Fran, which caused the Potomac River to rise fifteen feet above flood level. Residents continued to cross the bridge for years after it was closed. In 1999, it was reopened, and then in 2010, it was transferred to new management.

The Forensic Science Center at Marshall University in Huntington, WV, began doing DNA relationship testing in December 2003.

HIDDEN IN
HALF MOON BAY

A House That Sam Built Mystery

(Preview of Book #2)

CINDY CLARK

1

NEW MOON

If this is a new moon, where did the old one go?

Thursday, July 27, 1995

Sam

Last thing Sam remembered, he was sound asleep in this lovely antique bed with his wife Anna and their two golden retrievers, Zeus and Zoey. He looked up and Zeus and Zoey's cute little heads were peering over the edge at him, cocked to the side, wondering. Wondering if he was playing with them.

He stared up at them. Sam could see they were contemplating jumping off the bed and making a puppy pile on the floor on top of him.

For the last twenty-four of his thirty years on this earth, Sam Bradley had no memory of ever falling out of bed. Even his darling wife had not had the occasion to push him out of bed since they had been married and sleeping together with the blessing of church and state.

Could the dogs have pushed him out of bed? Sam didn't think they were that strong, even if they worked together. The dogs didn't appear to be alarmed. Not very comforting, however, since he had recently encountered instances where they failed to demonstrate alarm when alarm was clearly warranted.

The antique bed was much higher than your normal bed. It was a black wrought-iron framed bed from the 1890s. The bed was located in an open loft of the cutest guest house in Half Moon Bay, California. Anna and Sam had been hired by the property owners to build a post and beam house overlooking the ocean. The bed had a little two-step stool to climb into it at the foot, making it nearly a three-foot drop to the floor. And it hurt when Sam fell out of it.

Sam did a quick inventory of his body for any injuries. Just sore. He stood up and inspected the bed. Maybe he and Anna had broken the bed. The dogs' tails were thump-thumping on top of Anna, who was still in bed. Sam walked around it, looking at the connection points and supports.

"What in God's name are you doing?" Anna asked sleepily.

"I just got thrown out of bed," Sam answered. "Before I crawl back in with you, I wanted to make sure the bed isn't broken."

"Feels fine to me," said Anna, who wiggled around a little. "If it is broken, I'm sure you can fix it, dear."

Sam wondered if that was a hint of sarcasm in her sleepy voice.

"What time is it, anyway?" she asked.

"Around four. Go back to sleep," Sam said.

Nothing was amiss with the bed that Sam could see. He thought of a couple of things they could do to make sure the bed was sturdy now that he was wide awake. But Anna looked like she needed a few more z's, so he let her sleep.

Sam headed down the stairs to make coffee. The first level was open concept. Kitchen and living room were all one room. There was a full bath with a shower that was part inside and part outside. It had a sliding glass door, which you could open if the weather was nice or close if it was cooler. Sam had never seen that configuration before for a shower. He wondered if snakes could get in that way. Snakes were his nemesis.

Upstairs in the loft, there was a half-bath, so you didn't

have to walk down the stairs in the dark if you had to go to the bathroom in the middle of the night. The house was maybe 700 square feet in total. A tiny house before tiny houses were even a thing. The living room had a two-story stone fireplace. The house had a wraparound deck so you could take in the view of the dramatic hills that towered over the house.

Much of the time, the house was right below the fog line. Sam and Anna were from Michigan, which occasionally had fog, but not like here. In Half Moon Bay, the fog was almost a daily occurrence. Thick, soupy fog that could last all day. Depending on the time of year, it might burn off by midmorning. But now, in July, it looked like this one was going to stick around most of the day.

Sam and Anna had arrived in Half Moon Bay several days ago after driving cross-country from Sam's parents' home in West Virginia. They just finished building them a log home overlooking the South Branch of the Potomac River. They met Lyle and Tabitha Kilpatrick through one of Sam's parents' neighbors. It took five days to drive cross-country with Zeus and Zoe, whom Sam and Anna referred to as the Z goldens. Sam drove his old work van and Anna drove their new four-wheel drive SUV.

They got a great deal on the SUV. It was a Mitsubishi, not very well known in the US yet. It sat up high, so it was great for driving off-road. But it handled well on the highway, too. Being from Michigan, Sam's father wanted to know why they didn't buy an American car, which were mostly made in Michigan. They test-drove a couple, but the cars didn't offer the same features at the price of the Mitsubishi. This made Sam a traitor to his Michigan neighbors. Sam wasn't planning to go back there. One more reason to avoid the state altogether.

Sam really wanted a Humvee like one of his friends from West Virginia had. This friend, Rob Livingston, was by far the coolest guy Sam had ever met. Like most men, Sam figured if he had his car, he would be cool, too. But the price tag was way too steep for the Bradley budget, and the inside was not made for hauling building supplies. It had this huge bump down the middle, with narrow, uncomfortable seats that only sat four people. Sam thought the back cargo bed would be big enough for a machine gun stand, if you had the need for that kind of thing. You definitely couldn't move scaffolding in the bed. Therefore, the Mitsubishi was practical and Sam, the home-state traitor, would learn to live with Humvee envy.

Lyle and Tabitha Kilpatrick were paying Sam and Anna what seemed at the time a king's ransom for the year to build this house. In West Virginia, Sam had wanted to rough it. They camped in tents while they were building the house. *Been there, done that*, thought Sam. Here, they got to stay in the gorgeous guest house.

This was Sam and Anna's first time on the Left Coast. The Kilpatricks told them they should work at their own pace and enjoy all that California had to offer. If the house was complete within twelve months, they would be happy. If it was finished sooner, they would still pay Sam and Anna the same amount. If unforeseen events caused delays beyond the year, they would pay extra by the month.

The landscape was so different from what they were used to in Michigan and West Virginia, like the eucalyptus trees that grew all over the Kilpatricks' one-hundred-acre property. The tree originated in Australia but grew mainly in the US in warm states like California and Texas. The Kilpatricks wanted to harvest some for the posts on the new house. The trees were denser than teak and grew straight, making them a perfect option. Lyle and Sam planned a leisurely walk later that day to mark some of the trees that might be usable. Lyle would then hire a tree service to take them down and haul them to the building site.

Sam took his coffee and went to sit on the porch. Zeus followed him out, but Zoey elected to stay snuggled up with Anna in the unbroken bed. It was still pitch black. The moon was just a sliver in the sky, visible when the fog parted for a few seconds. Coyotes howled in the distance, and foxes yipped closer to the house. Zeus's ears were twitching with each unfamiliar sound.

Sam watched for the sunrise over the hills in this strange country. The house was set way off the road at the end of a five-mile private driveway. *Good thing it didn't snow here*, Sam thought. The average temperatures were between 50 and 70 degrees all year round. Occasionally, it got slightly warmer than 70, but the house didn't have air conditioning. Nor did it have window screens. No bugs, Sam was told. He would have to see that to believe it. *Bet they had all manner of big, ugly poisonous snakes, though.*

Sam thought he saw a movement at the tree line. If this had been West Virginia, he would have been reaching for his shotgun. They ran into some rather unfriendly neighbors there that had murdered several people and stashed their bodies on his parents' property. Those neighbors were immensely displeased that new owners were taking up residence, and the last nine months had Sam and Anna on edge with threats to property and person. As a for-instance, Sam was shot in the ass with a hunting arrow during a snowstorm. He was looking forward to an adrenaline-free build in sunny-ish, laid-back

California. In any case, California state laws prohibited him from bringing his gun to California, so he left it back in West Virginia for his parents. Here in California, Sam had no reason to think that the movement he saw was not caused by the ordinary wildlife, more afraid of him than he was of them.

Sam was a pretty big guy. Six feet tall, 180 pounds. Brown hair kept kinda shaggy. He had been working construction for about ten years. He stood up and roared into the darkness. Figured that would scare off whatever was lurking at the tree line.

He reached down to take hold of Zeus's collar to make sure Zeus didn't chase after whatever animal might be returning to its den at daybreak. Sam understood that mountain lions and bobcats had occasionally been sighted (those he did not care to see) and feral donkeys, which he wouldn't mind seeing at some point. He did not, however, relish the thought of chasing after Zeus pre-dawn on a doggie mission to bring down this unknown animal.

Feeling particularly foolish for roaring at shadows, Sam went back inside to get a second cup of coffee. He was glad the closest neighbor was miles away. *Way to make a great impression on the new neighborhood.* He grabbed a blanket before he went back out to the porch because the fog was damp. He remembered hearing something somebody famous once said: "The coldest winter I ever spent was a summer in San Francisco." Clearly, the guy wasn't from Michigan, but it did feel more like fall than the end of July.

Anna came out onto the porch just after it got light. She had on a tank top and boxer shorts and was covered by a blanket that dragged behind her, Zoey chasing after it. Anna settled down in the Adirondack chair next to Sam. Zoey curled up on the corner of the blanket. You could hear the waves of the Pacific Ocean hitting the beach about two miles away, as the crow flew.

"Did you fix the bed?" she asked.

"You want to head on back inside and see?" Sam asked.

Lyle drove up to the cottage in an old Land Rover, great for driving off-road. Lyle was taller than Sam, six-three or so. He was in his late fifties with sandy blond hair with no gray showing. Looked like Lyle might still have six-pack abs. He told Sam he was retired from the FBI. Sam had asked him what he did, but Lyle initiated complex evasion tactics. Lyle was friends with some of Sam's friends back in West Virginia who did the same thing when asked about their jobs. So, Sam knew better than to ask again.

Sam suggested they cover the property on foot, making it easier to see the trees. Lyle was carrying a day backpack and wearing hiking boots and cargo pants. A black t-shirt rounded out his ensemble.

In contrast, Sam was wearing baggy jeans, an old t-shirt with a Little Feat band logo covered by Sam's second-best flannel shirt worn unbuttoned, and old white sneakers speckled with paint and concrete.

They started at the top of the property, at the highest point where the house was going to be. It was the area with the least amount of old-growth trees, so it was explorable in quick order.

The house site wasn't going to be at the very summit because there was a requirement that the house not be visible from Highway 1. The house had to sit down a little lower but would still have panoramic views of the Pacific Ocean. It was also going to be just above the fog line, so the valley could be buried in fog, but the house would look like it was floating in the clouds.

The hike to the very top was moderately steep but didn't require any gear. If you leaned forward, you could reach out and almost touch the ground. At one point, Lyle put up his hand and motioned for them to stop. Out of his backpack, he pulled some binoculars, professional grade. *Maybe he got to take them with him when he retired from the FBI*, Sam thought. Lyle trained them on a point in the distance. He smiled as he handed them to Sam and pointed in the direction of some scrub brush.

Sam adjusted the focus on the binoculars, not knowing what to look for. Then he saw a small herd of feral donkeys, descendants of abandoned livestock that roamed the sparsely populated hills from the coast all the way to Palo Alto, ripping down fencing and causing property damage.

Sam couldn't resist. He had somewhat of a reputation as a funny guy, but he was still feeling out his audience.

"Hey, Lyle, what do you call an overweight, miniature, three-legged donkey with only one eye and a flatulence problem?" Sam asked.

"Why do I have a feeling you are going to tell me no matter what I say?" Lyle said.

"I suppose if you said I was fired, I might not tell you, but guaranteed, the need to know the answer will eat at you all day," said Sam, grinning.

Lyle just stood there looking at Sam with one eyebrow raised.

"All right, then," said Sam. "It's a dinky, stinky, winky, chunky, wonky donkey."

"Bet you don't often have the opportunity to trot out that joke," said Lyle. "You are going to be quite the hit with your kids when you and Anna get around to it."

"We're working on it," said Sam.

Lyle chuckled, and they moved on. Sam made a mental note to rein in his humor around Lyle. If Lyle enjoyed that kind of humor, Sam would have expected him to reciprocate with his own limerick or joke. Sam knew not everyone wanted to play with him at that level. Including Anna, who did not like to kid around. But he loved her anyway.

The two men stopped at the highest ridge to enjoy the ocean views, then walked toward the northern property line.

"I heard on the radio on the ride over that there was an earthquake early this morning. The epicenter was forty miles north of San Francisco, but I understand from the announcers that it could be felt as far south as San Jose. Did you feel anything?" asked Lyle.

"What time did it happen?" Sam asked.

"Around 4 a.m.," Lyle said.

"Huh, then maybe I did. I was thrown out of bed onto the floor. I just thought it was Anna."

"That rolling movement can do that to you."

At first, Sam thought Lyle might have cameras hidden in the guesthouse and was spying on his and Anna's nighttime activities. But then he realized his mistake. Lyle didn't mean Anna; he meant the earthquake. Duh.

"Wow, my first earthquake," said Sam.

"Let's hope it is your last, too. The big Loma Prieta earthquake in '89 affected this area pretty hard. That one hit near Santa Cruz, south of here. Big one. Magnitude 6.9. A lot of people died, and thousands were injured. This one was small in comparison. A 2.4, I think they said."

"Yikes. Tell me again why you wanted to move here?" *Welcome to California.*

"I don't know any place that doesn't have challenges with Mother Nature. Hurricanes, tornadoes, snow and ice storms, dust storms, wildfires."

"I suppose you're right. I'm not sure where Anna and I will end up after we have satisfied our wanderlust." *Did he just say wanderlust? Must have hit his head when he fell out of bed,* Sam thought.

They descended into the fog again and moved toward the first stand of tall trees. A couple of trees were the right height and diameter. The smell of eucalyptus was intoxicating with the leaves crunching underfoot. Lyle reached into his bag and pulled out some yellow tape. He banded the trees and made handwritten notes in his notebook on their location.

Just on the other side of the trees, they saw something neither of them could have ever possibly imagined.

Thank you for reading!

Go to *cindyclarkauthor.com* for more books in the *A House That Sam Built Mystery* Series, including the second book, *Hidden in Half Moon Bay*.

If you enjoyed this book, please review it online!